WHO IS THE KILLER?

SIR AMYAS DANCER
The head of the family, whose bizarre plans to build a Roman amphitheater led him straight to Katherine's body?

CARLETON DANCER
Amyas's son and a former rock star, who now collects buttons such as those on the dead girl's blouse?

MRS. LARKIN
The loyal family retainer who loathes being called a servant—and who saw right through Miss Katherine St. Croix?

DAVID PROCTOR
The young poet whose regard for the Dancers may not be as pure as it seems?

CASSANDRA DANCER
Amyas's daughter, determined to marry David Proctor—whatever the cost?

A DEATH FOR A DANCER

E. X. Giroux

BALLANTINE BOOKS • NEW YORK

Library of Congress Catalog Card Number: 85-10896

ISBN 0-345-33408-6

This edition published by arrangement with St. Martin's Press

Manufactured in the United States of America

First Ballantine Books Edition: November 1986

This book is for
Maureen and Dimitrios Nikas

CHAPTER ONE

Willis Seton possessed a number of favorable attributes—a professional competence, a portly, reassuring appearance, and a resonant voice. He had one drawback—a loquacity that could be alarming, at times irritating, and once in a while, amusing.

Generally Robert Forsythe found the solicitor amusing and for the first twenty minutes of the monologue had exercised patience. For a time Seton conversed about his new office, pointing to each improvement and enlarging upon it. Forsythe had murmured compliments about the amount of space, the dazzling expanse of glass, the thick wall-to-wall carpeting, and the well-fitted bar cunningly concealed in paneling. Forsythe was relieved that his secretary, Miss Sanderson, couldn't see Seton's office. She was becoming increasingly insistent about moving from their own cramped chambers in a centuries-old structure into something like this in one of the new buildings springing up all over London.

When Seton abandoned this subject, Forsythe leaned forward hopefully only to find himself listening to details on the Seton family, particularly the birth of a new grandson.

Weather followed the Seton saga, unseasonal as always for the month of July.

He started to squirm and Seton promptly returned to his first topic. "Can't see, my boy, why you don't chuck those chambers of yours. Know they were your father's, and his, but time to move on. Shouldn't think they're even healthy."

"I like them."

Seton gave a chuckle that appeared to work its way up from his sizable paunch. "What do you like—mildewed walls, smoky hearths, steps leading up and down for no apparent reason?"

"I like the feel of it."

Hard to explain, Forsythe mused, what that feeling was exactly. The old building did have noticeable defects but the atmosphere seemed eminently suitable for the practice of law. The narrow corridors and poky rooms had an odor of ancient parchment, leather, and smoke from long-perished pipes. The smell in Seton's building was positively antiseptic. The solicitor was settling back comfortably and before he could release another barrage of words, Forsythe said, "You *did* ask to see me, Willis."

Seton chuckled again. "In other words, get to the point. You young chaps aren't long on patience. I thought Miss Sanderson might have filled you in. You're a lucky man, Robert. Wish I could lay my hands on a legal secretary like her. Remember when she first came to work for your father—"

Hastily, Forsythe broke in. "Sandy didn't seem to have a clear idea about the problem."

"Can't see why not. This Dancer case, as the newspapers are calling it, has been on front pages for a fortnight."

"I'm just back from abroad and Sandy has been on vacation. All I know is that the murdered body of a girl was found on the Dancer property. And, of course, that Sir Amyas wishes to retain my services."

"Wrong on one point. The St. Croix female was a

woman, not a girl. The Dancers, and the police at first, thought she was in her early twenties. Turned out she would never have seen thirty again. St. Croix wasn't her name either. She passed herself off as Katherine St. Croix but she was born Katerina Padrinski.'' Pushing himself up, he opened a filing cabinet and started flipping through folders. Fine looking man, Forsythe thought, overweight but not gross, a mane of snowy hair, a wide florid face. ''Ah, here we are.'' The solicitor plumped a fat manila envelope down in front of Forsythe.

Forsythe hefted it. ''Seems a lot of material.''

''Copies of police reports and a bunch of background material. Thought it might help you understand the Dancers.''

''I suppose Sir Amyas has been charged.'' For a man of many words Seton's answer was incredibly brief, simply a negative jerk of the leonine head. ''One of his family?''

''No charge been laid as yet. Young fellow was called in to help with the investigation—minor villain and a known associate of the St. Croix or Padrinski woman, who was something of a villain herself. Understand he's cleared himself with an alibi for the time of the woman's murder.''

Forsythe's hand fell away from the heavy envelope and he raised his brows. ''Then what in the devil did you call me in for? Until a charge is laid, a barrister is about as much use as a pen without ink.''

The solicitor's eyes avoided the younger man's. ''Sir Amyas is most determined. You would have to know the man to understand that he doesn't request, he orders; have to know the relationship between the Dancers and Setons to understand why I jump when he yells. My family acted as stewards for the Dancer family as far back as their history goes. It was grandfather who finally tried to break loose from them. Got a legacy from a cousin who emigrated to Australia and did rather well and had my father educated as a solicitor.''

3

Forsythe smiled. "It would appear your grandfather wasn't successful."

"Shamed to admit it, Robert, but no. Father inherited Sir Crawford Dancer and when my turn came I got his son Amyas. Only difference is that instead of counting livestock and collecting rents for the Dancers, the Setons now handle their legal affairs and fish them out of the most astounding messes." He fingered his thick hair. "Still pulling the old forelock and saying 'yes sir,' 'no sir.'"

"That doesn't explain why Sir Amyas has his heart set on a barrister when—"

"Doesn't want a barrister. Wants a private investigator." Forsythe's mouth snapped open and the solicitor raised a hand and continued. "Don't get your back up. It's your own fault, young Robert. Getting your picture in the papers and accounts of the cases you've solved. Know what the news lads are calling you? 'Mission Impossible' Forsythe!"

Forsythe's normally pale face was now as ruddy as Seton's. "Bunch of asses! Certainly I've been pulled into a few cases, but not of my own volition. Either I've been on the scene or someone I know has been involved. I practice law and *that* is quite enough to keep me occupied. Surely you've put Sir Amyas onto a good private inquiry agent?"

"Tried to. Chap who was formerly an inspector with the C.I.D. has undertaken confidential investigations and he's reliable. Sir Amyas wouldn't hear of it. Wants you. Says he always gets the best. Compliment, young Robert."

"Not to me it isn't." Forsythe stood up. "Give him my regrets and tell him I'm not available. Tell him if he doesn't want an investigator, to put his trust in the police. They'll get to the bottom of it."

"Doubt with this one they will. It's distinctly weird. Much like the people involved. Didn't want to do this but it looks like I must. In the past I've done some good turns for you, haven't I?"

Sinking slowly back into the armchair, Forsythe stared at

his friend. Willis Seton had indeed done some good turns. At one point in his career when he desperately needed friends, Seton had come to his assistance and stood staunchly by. "That goes without saying. Are you about to present the fee?"

The solicitor had the grace to look abashed. "Said I didn't want to do this. Not asking you to take the case. Only asking you to see Sir Amyas, listen to him, and tell *him* you won't do it."

"More or less get you off the hook, eh?"

"Exactly. Case of the messenger who brings the bad news. You won't have to see him again. Me . . . I'm stuck with the Dancers for life."

"Very well. Sandy and I will drive up, hear him out, and politely suggest your retired inspector." Forsythe was on his feet again. He picked up the envelope. "I'm curious, Willis. Are you afraid of this man?"

"Afraid?" The leonine head shook. "Feel a sense of responsibility. Suppose it's habitual." His eyes seemed to see a procession of shadowy Seton ancestors serving shadowy Dancers. "And this family . . . done the most outrageous, ridiculous, godawful things. To put it mildly, they're terribly eccentric people. Yet . . ." His eyes returned to his colleague. "When you know more about them you'll think I'm gaga myself but, Robert, the Dancers are innocents."

CHAPTER TWO

"**I**NNOCENTS," MISS SANDERSON SAID SCATHINGLY. SHE was curled up on the Rover's leather seat beside Forsythe, a black briefcase resting in her lap. "Willis Seton must be fast approaching senility if he hasn't already reached it."

Forsythe took his eyes off the road long enough to cast an approving look at his secretary. She looked quite fetching in a dark green linen suit and a lighter green silk shirt. To protect her freshly styled gray hair she'd bound green chiffon around it. "Willis did mention the Dancers are eccentric."

She snorted and thumped the briefcase. "More like bizarre."

"Past or present?"

"Didn't you read any of the material he gave us?"

"Only the police reports of the murder. Hardly seemed worth it to wade through that lot when all we're going to do is say 'no,' kindly but firmly."

"That at least is a blessing. Anyone who gets mixed up with this bunch seems to end up just as weird." She zipped open the case and extracted a thick sheaf of typewritten pages. "Care to have a history lesson?"

"Sounds dull but it will help wile away the time."

Her face was as austere as usual but her eyes glinted with wicked amusement. "The Dancer house is called the Priory. Seems an ancestor, early on, booted out an order of monks and took the building for his own. Named the lake behind it Priory Lake. Original chap. A century or so later his descendant decided the Priory was tumbling around his ears and built the present house. The name was retained."

Forsythe yawned. "Maybe I'll skip the history."

"I'll give you a few highlights. Sir Harold Dancer followed his king on the Crusades. When Harold got home he found his lady dallying with a man-at-arms. He drugged the lady, beat the unfortunate lover to death, quartered him, and slipped him into bed with the sleeping girl." Miss Sanderson shook her head. "What an awakening that must have been."

"What was the lady's reaction?"

"Doesn't say here but she lived to a ripe old age and gave Sir Harold a number of children. How's that for innocents?"

"The punishment for adultery in those days was swift and barbaric." He pointed to a road sign. "Ah, the county of Cheshire. Nice, isn't it?"

"Idyllic. Either Constable or Turner or a little of each." She looked with delight at the verdant countryside, the gentle slopes and thick hedges guarding the roadside. "One of these days I'm going to invest in a cottage in a place like this. I've always longed to live in the country."

"I thought you were raised in a village."

Miss Sanderson shrugged a green linen shoulder. "Born not raised. Father was a country parson with more children than income. I was farmed out to a childless aunt and uncle and raised in London. Yes, I long for a cottage, a garden, flowers. I could get away from the maddening crowds—"

"I believe that's madding, Sandy."

"—and grow vegetables and—"

7

"'And a small cabin build there, of clay and wattles made: Nine bean rows—'"

"Robby!"

"Sorry. It's only that my imagination is strained by picturing you in a rural setting."

"Perhaps right now. Later on, after I retire . . ."

Forsythe vainly tried to picture life without Miss Sanderson. He couldn't remember his mother but from his earliest days there had always been Sandy. To him she'd been all, a mother, an older sister, at times a conscience. "There's always the old manse in Sussex."

"That's yours. I want some little corner of my own." Sharp blue eyes veered toward him. "And I know what you're up to. Trying to avoid your history lesson. Won't work. Where was I?"

"Sir Harold the Crusader."

Paper rattled. "We move on in time. Shortly after the American Civil War, Sir Charles Dancer, who greatly admired the Confederacy, had the entire front of his Elizabethan home covered with a facade. Reproduced an antebellum home from the deep South complete with pillars and balconies and a gallant effort at wisteria. He was more successful with that than with his retainers who balked at calling him the ole massah. While Sir Charles was on his deathbed his son, who had sympathized with the North, had carpenters in to rip down the facade. Sir Charles died to the sound of saws and hammers."

Forsythe drew the car up beside a signpost and eyed it doubtfully. Impatiently, Miss Sanderson pointed left and Forsythe steered the car onto a narrower road. The Rover rattled over a humpbacked bridge and Miss Sanderson selected another sheet of paper. "You're going to love this one. Turn of this century and Sir Godfrey Dancer. Never went to the mysterious East in his life but acquired a passion for the Orient. Built on the shore of Priory Lake a miniature

8

Chinese temple and promptly renamed the lake the China Sea. Called the temple Mandalay. To give it atmosphere he came up with an Oriental gentleman who claimed to be a spiritual descendant of Confucius and was called Confucius Again. Robby, will you stop that?"

Forsythe, who had been softly humming, now broke into riotous song. "'On the road to Mandalay, where the flying fishes play, and—'"

"Will you shut up! Robby, this temple played a part in the murder of Katherine St. Croix."

"I told you I read the police reports."

"Confucius Again," his secretary continued doggedly, "moved in with Sir Godfrey and his family, donned exotic robes, and converted his patron to an odd blend of Eastern mysticism and religion. The locals were rather used to the Dancer family and raised no objections until the baronet, spurred by Confucius Again, decided to convert *them*. There were screams of idolatry and paganism and the populace led by—"

"Beginning to sound like the closing scene from the old Frankenstein movie. Remember the torchlight parade to the evil castle?"

"Wasn't far short of it. The locals were led by clergy and Sir Godfrey's son Cuthbert who happened to be a devout Lutheran. Sir Godfrey prepared to repel them and armed all his manservants. Seems his second passion was collecting antique weapons and seeing they were all he had in hand he surrounded his temple with guards brandishing cutlasses, blunderbusses, and battle-axes."

"Good Lord!"

"For his own weapon Sir Godfrey chose a crossbow. The avenging mob arrived to find Confucius Again waiting on the steps of the temple hoping to overcome their bloody-mindedness with words of peace. He was immediately recognized by a cabinet maker from Chester. Seems the

Oriental sage was none other than Jimmy Chang, formerly an employee of a Chinese laundry. Incensed by this duplicity Sir Godfrey turned his ire and his crossbow not on the mob but on Confucius Again."

"I rather hope Sir Godfrey's aim was true, Sandy."

"He missed his target but the whole affair ended tragically. Sir Godfrey had a stroke of apoplexy and fell dead on the spot. His son, now Sir Cuthbert, overcome by remorse reacted as a true Dancer."

"Let me guess. Cuthbert renounced his own religion and converted to Buddhism or whatever."

"As a detective you have the makings of a barrister. No, but he insisted his father should be buried as befitting an Oriental gentleman. He had the body laid out in a Chinese robe and had workmen in to turn Mandalay into a crypt. Two cement box affairs were installed to receive the coffins of Sir Godfrey and Lady Dancer, who at that time was very much alive. Cuthbert also bought, at great expense, four jade statuettes, one white, one green, and two pink. After his father's body was installed in the crypt, Cuthbert had some runes put over the door. They were carved in Chinese characters but were more Egyptian in content. A curse on any who defiled the tomb. Cuthbert's mother seems to have been strong-minded and refused to be interred with her husband; she was buried instead in the Harper graveyard with the other Dancers. A huge padlock with only one key was put on Mandalay's door and until recently the crypt was never entered."

"Until Katherine St. Croix was found there."

"Exactly." Neatly aligning the edges of the papers, Miss Sanderson tucked them back into the case. "I've only touched on a few anecdotes from the history of the family. It makes lively reading."

The Rover had reached another crossroads. Without glancing at the signpost, the barrister asked, "Which way, Sandy?"

"Left."

"You're amazing. Did you memorize that map?"

"Merely glanced at it," she said airily. "But when we get to Harper you're on your own. There's such a maze of lanes around it, I can't figure where the Priory is. Robby, I'm starving. Do you suppose the Dancers will feed us?"

"We can hardly expect bed and breakfast from people we're going to turn down cold."

"To say nothing of firmly and gently. Want more history to wile away the time?"

"Do you have any more recent?"

"Loads. What do you know about Sir Amyas and his household?"

"Very little. At the Priory are his two children and his father-in-law, and two sisters live on the estate too."

"Let me fill you in. Sir Amyas married twice. His first wife—"

He glanced at the briefcase. "Aren't you going to rustle more paper?"

"Don't need to. To get back to Sir Amyas. I suppose I should start at the beginning."

"Do try to condense it, Sandy."

"The baronet inherited a large chunk of money but it appears Sir Amyas allows money to slip through his fingers. Always has some project going that's not only time-consuming but money-consuming. But at the time of his first marriage he still had enough assets to marry for love. His first wife was a Lady Amanda Gore-Carleton, strong on blue blood and short on cash. She promptly gave her husband a son and a couple of years later choked to death on a wishbone—"

"Surely you mean fishbone."

"Uh, uh. She was delicately nibbling meat from a wishbone, sucked it back into her windpipe, and expired. By this time Sir Amyas was feeling the financial pinch. A year later he took to his bosom a seventeen-year-old girl, Viola Gillimede, daughter of a wealthy industrialist. Horace Gillimede gave his new son-in-law a handsome marriage settlement that not only solved his current money crisis but promised more of the same in the future.''

"It sounds as though this Dancer lands on his feet."

"Sir Amyas does but in the strangest ways. His plans for living off his father-in-law came to disaster shortly before Viola presented him with a daughter. Horace Gillimede was a hardheaded businessman, far more interested in his firm than his family. One day he came home unexpectedly and caught his wife having fun and games with a young Welsh boxer. Horace drove the erring pair from his door and they made their getaway in the boxer's car. Outside of Liverpool their car was hit broadside by a lorry and Mrs. Gillimede and her lover died.

"Horace was not only filled with remorse but something else that wasn't recognized at the time. He had a complete mental collapse. Seems he blamed himself for his wife's fall from grace, thought he'd neglected her for his business. To atone he liquified all his holdings and gave his money away—"

"Did you say *gave*, Sandy?"

"Every last pound. To religious organizations and charities. When he was suitably broke he returned to Sir Amyas and Lady Dancer in sackcloth and ashes to pay penitence for his sins for the rest of his life. So, Sir Amyas was not only stuck with a mad father-in-law but with a wife he apparently couldn't stand."

"Did Viola Dancer also conveniently choke on a wishbone?"

"She drowned in Priory Lake or, as it's now called, the China Sea. But that was only a year ago, so Sir Amyas endured her company for about a quarter of a century."

Despite himself, Forsythe was becoming interested in the

Dancers. "I understand Sir Amyas is a fabulously wealthy man."

"He has the oddest luck. Before his second marriage Sir Amyas decided to run an experiment. He bought a ranch in western Canada and proceeded to try to cross Highland cattle with bison. Apparently he figured not only deer and antelope still roam the range but also buffalo. It didn't work and he rented the ranch to a man who was content to raise Herefords. Sir Amyas returned to England and promptly forgot about it. Shortly after Horace Gillimede gave away his money the tenant rancher decided to sink a new well. What came spouting up was black."

Forsythe chuckled. "He'd struck oil."

"He had indeed and the proceeds flowed into the Dancer coffers. This enabled Sir Amyas to continue happily with his harebrained schemes. Some of them have been dandies. Robby, turn right at this next crossroads."

The barrister obeyed, swinging the wheel and piloting the Rover to the right. "From that grin you're wearing, Sandy, I take it you have a favorite."

Miss Sanderson's smile broadened. "I've taken a fancy to the Great Fox Hunt Saga."

"Fox hunt? I'm not terribly taken with the sport but it sounds harmless."

"Not Sir Amyas' version. This happened five years ago and at that time his passion had turned to nudity—in a wholesome way, sun and health and bodybuilding and that sort of thing. He'd joined a nudist association in London and was trying to get permission to turn the Priory into a nudist colony. The residents of Harper and the surrounding district fought him tooth and nail. They won and Sir Amyas was out of luck. He didn't take his defeat tamely. He organized a fox hunt, complete with outriders, hounds, and horns."

"Tallyho and shades of John Peel, eh?"

"Except for one detail. The hunt pelted all over the district, ending with a triumphant ride up the high street in Harper with Sir Amyas in the lead."

Miss Sanderson dissolved into helpless laughter and Forsythe said with a smile, "I can guess the rest. The hunters were from his nudist club."

Miss Sanderson sputtered and reached into her outsize handbag for a tissue. She wiped at streaming eyes. "All any of them, including Sir Amyas, was wearing were riding boots and derby hats. Harper is a staid little place with staid inhabitants, and their relations with the Dancers since that hunt have been distinctly cool. Robby, I can *see* that ride up the high street."

"Our baronet must have broken innumerable laws with the hunt."

"He did but one of his dearest friends happens to be the chief constable. As usual the Dancers came out unscathed."

"Are the rest of the family as colorful?"

"Not all of them. Sir Amyas' sisters, both older than he, appear to be quiet ladies. Miss Sybil and Miss Arabella are still personae gratae in Harper. His daughter Cassandra, now twenty-one, was educated in Switzerland, though she went to a convent school in Italy for a time. She did spend some months on a commune in the States but that's not unusual. Horace Gillimede only ventures off the estate to attend protest rallies. He turns up waving placards and ranting about salvation. Sounds fairly harmless."

"Horace also sounds like that bearded prophet at the funeral in Bury-Sutton."

All signs of amusement left his secretary's face, leaving it closed and cold. Miss Sanderson still hadn't recovered from their experiences in that town. "Similar," she said tersely and continued. "Sir Amyas' son and heir, Gore-Carleton, mercifully known as Carleton or Carl, seems to have inherited his father's tendencies. Carleton has traveled a

14

great deal, done a number of crazy things, but the highlight of his life thus far has been the rock group he organized and led. It was called Carl and His Cannibals and they had rather a ghastly gimmick. During their performances they threw dismembered parts of bodies into the ranks of fans. Arms and legs and heads. Made of plastic and papier-mâché but Carleton insisted on the look of authenticity and they cost a bundle to make up. The expense eventually broke up their act."

"Thanks to the merciful God. How old is this chap?"

"Twenty-eight."

"What's he up to now?"

"After his group broke up he returned to the Priory and for the last year has devoted his life to collecting buttons."

"*Buttons?*"

"According to Willis Seton, buttons. Incidentally, Robby, I think Willis deserves a hero's medal for trying to handle this bunch of maniacs." She patted her flat stomach. "I'm *starved*."

"You're the navigator. How much farther to Harper?"

"Down this twisty lane and we should arrive at the high street. Ah, there it is. My! Talk about stepping into the past, shades of Merry Olde England."

As the car rumbled over cobblestones Forsythe silently agreed. The village looked like an old print. A narrow street was flanked by half-timbered buildings housing small shops. The chemist shop bore red and green globes in its window and the signs, flapping in the breeze, were almost illegible. "All that's needed, Sandy, is a coach drawn by spanking horses. Ah, there's the Harper Arms. Care to stop?"

"You'd better; my stomach is complaining audibly." Getting out of the car onto a narrow walk, she peered up at the faded sign. "Prop. M. Bantam. Tom Jones land." She swung around toward her companion. "Let me tell you what we'll find inside. Genuine beams, dark old furniture, sloping floors—"

"Don't get your hopes up, Sandy. Could be tarted up with chrome and imitation leather and tankards from Japan."

"—and hunting prints and a fireplace large enough to roast an ox. Want to bet?"

"I no longer bet with you. Good way to lose money. Let's have a look."

It took a few moments for their eyes to adjust from sunlight to the dim interior. Forsythe blinked and was heartily glad he hadn't bet. Not only was it as Sandy had described but the barmaid, polishing glass behind the counter, *was* straight out of Tom Jones. She had a mass of dark curls, a jovial expression, and a buxom figure. Leaning majestically on an elbow watching a checker game was the proprietor. M. Bantam fit the decor perfectly. He too was stout, running greatly to stomach, which was covered by a checkered waistcoat. The only other people in the room were the two elderly checker players.

Four pairs of eyes swiveled to inspect the arrivals and M. Bantam moved with stately grace to a position behind shining taps. He made them welcome in a deep baritone, allowed it was a fine day, and asked what their pleasure was.

"Nut brown ale," Miss Sanderson breathed.

"Two pints of bitter," Forsythe said hastily.

The pints were duly drawn. The landlord apologized for the brew, mentioned he thought the last lot of bitter might have had a bit too much air, watched them sample it, and beamed when both declared it good. Queried about food he admitted, after some thought, the missus could come up with a mixed grill. Lowering his voice he confided, "My suggestion is bread and cheese. Missus is a dab hand with bread and it's straight out of the oven. Got a nice chunk of aged Cheshire." Leaning over the counter, he tapped the older checker player lightly on a bald head. "Stop your ogling, Bob," he roared. Both Forsythe and his secretary started and Mr. Bantam said in a lower tone, "Old Bob's coming up ninety-five and stone deaf but still got an eye for a likely lass."

Miss Sanderson, who could scarcely be considered a lass, pinkened with pleasure, and without consulting her companion ordered bread and cheese. They carried their drinks to a seat resembling a church pew and deposited the glasses on a table.

"Bread and cheese doesn't sound like much of a meal, Sandy."

"When in Tom Jones land one must have nut brown ale and bread and cheese. Wish you'd bet with me."

"I'm not Horace Gillimede and I don't give my money away. Ah, here comes lunch."

The plump barmaid deposited a platter before them bearing a crusty loaf of warm bread, sweet country butter, and a huge chunk of cheese. More bitters arrived and they proceeded to stuff themselves. It was tasty and more than substantial. When the plates were removed their host stepped over to ask how they'd fared. Behind his broad back old Bob winked a rheumy eye at Miss Sanderson and gave her a lecherous toothless grin. Miss Sanderson smiled back.

"Could you tell us," Forsythe asked, "where the Priory is located?"

Bantam's shrewd eyes gave them a closer scrutiny and then he allowed he could do that. He gave lengthy and detailed instructions. Forsythe paid no attention. His human computer, Miss Sanderson, was storing the information away in her memory bank. Bantam had the necessary quota of human curiosity. He stuck out a big hand and announced, "Matthew Bantam, at your service."

Forced into a declaration, Forsythe shook the hand and said, "Miss Abigail Sanderson and Robert Forsythe."

"Not my place to ask, Mr. Forsythe, but will you be staying at those Dancers' house?"

"I'm inclined to doubt it."

"Long drive back to London."

While Forsythe was agreeing, he wondered how the devil Bantam had figured that out. Bantam rubbed his lowest chin. "Got a couple of nice rooms here. Clean and comfortable. Missus is a fair to middling cook. No choice, have to take what she has a mind to put together. Got a snuggery back there you could use for meals. Get you away from the crowds." He waved a hand at the checker players as though there were standing room only.

"We'll probably be here only one night," Forsythe told him.

"Might's well be comfortable. Place up the street takes in boarders but rooms are cupboard size." He lowered his voice. "W.C. outside in the yard, too. Willing to give you special rates." He named an amount that hardly sounded Tom Jonesish.

The barrister glanced at his secretary but she was dreamily eyeing a dim hunting print. "Sounds fine."

"See to them rooms." Turning away he caught the older checker player in the act. "Get them eyes off the lass!" he roared at old Bob.

Forsythe grinned and turned to Miss Sanderson. "You're playing hell with Bob's concentration."

"And mine host is playing hell with your wallet," she retorted.

"At least you won't have to run out in the night air to locate the w.c. Mr. Bantam's ancestors were probably pirates but one night won't break me."

She stood up and picked up her large handbag. The clasp was large too, a shiny brass grill-like ornament. She touched the clasp. "Want me to use the snooper when we get to the Priory?"

18

"I doubt it. Use your own judgment."

"Thank God for electronics. No more writer's cramp taking notes."

At the door Miss Sanderson turned to wave a hand at her admirer. Old Bob enthusiastically waved back.

CHAPTER THREE

SETTLING BEHIND THE WHEEL, FORSYTHE ASKED, "WHERE away, navigator?"

"Further up the high street until we reach the church. There it is. What a beauty! Wonder how old it is."

"Possibly fourteenth century." Forsythe slowed to admire the structure. The gentle slope around it was covered with moss-encrusted tombstones, tilting and tottering, bearing witness to other, perhaps gentler, days.

Miss Sanderson touched his arm. "That white Victorian house dead ahead. Turn there."

They turned onto a lane. The cobblestones trailed off and the Rover's tires hit gravel first and then a dirt surface. A few widely spaced houses lounged to their right in the July sun. To their left was a row of high-shouldered, narrow, attached houses. Miss Sanderson pointed at the end one. "That's the home of the Widow Hawkins who takes in boarders. Turn there."

"How do you garner all these details so quickly?"

"I have to. You never listen to directions. Mine host told me there was a stone lion on the lawn. Observe the noble beast. The reason I know it's his competition is because of the sign in one of the front windows. Hey, look at that."

He followed her pointing finger. "The widow has a neat garden and what looks like a tool shed. What's so startling?"

"What's missing. Nary a sign of the outside w.c. that Bantam warned us about."

The barrister laughed. "Propaganda, my dear Sandy. A neat way of steering people away from the competition. Any more turns?"

"None. There are the gate posts of the estate. It's practically on the doorstep of Harper. Half a mile from these posts to the house." Miss Sanderson cast a disgusted look from her window. "Blimey, but this is a mess."

"Unkempt, but then it would take an army of gardeners to keep a place this size under cultivation. Probably it will be better around the house."

It wasn't. The Elizabethan house looked forlornly across a sea of tangled grass and wild bushes. The drive slashed through it like a riverbed through a ravine. Drawing the car up before the front entrance Forsythe got out, circled the car, and opened the door for his secretary. A stiff breeze rippled through the tall grass, bending their heads. It playfully tugged at the chiffon over Miss Sanderson's gray hair and she reknotted the scarf under her chin. For a time they stared up at the house. It seemed as neglected as the grounds. Touching his companion's arm, Forsythe led the way up the shallow steps. The knocker, green with verdigris, had hardly thumped the oaken panel before the door jerked open and a young woman bolted out. "David, you're late!" She skidded to a stop and stared accusingly at them. "You're not David."

Forsythe admitted this and gave her their names. They didn't appear to interest her and she stared over his shoulder. Miss Sanderson was running glacial eyes up and down the girl. From the neck up she wasn't eyecatching at all. Her face was round with a pug nose and eyes set too close together. Straw-colored pigtails stuck out stiffly from her head. From the neck down was a different matter. She wore a flesh-colored body stocking under what looked like a pink bikini. The figure revealed was not spectacular but more than adequate.

The barrister cleared his throat and without removing her eyes from the drive the girl told him, "You're wasting your time. We never buy at the door."

"We're not peddlars," Forsythe told her amiably. "Willis Seton sent us."

"Willy? Oh, Amy will know all about that. There David is now!" She ran past Forsythe and down the steps. "Where have you been? You can't put inspiration on hold, David."

The man drew the bike to a wobbling stop, dismounted, and bent to remove the clip from a gray flannel trouser leg. This should have been a simple operation but the girl had cast herself upon him and was clinging like a limpet. Firmly he detached her, snapped off the clip, and straightened. "You can't fight fate or this broken-down bike. Ruddy thing blew a tire and I had to push it back into Harper to have it mended. Who are your guests?"

"They aren't guests. They've come to see Amy."

"Manners," the young man chided. "And introductions, Cass."

She waved a hand. "Mrs. Sanders and Mr. Foster."

"Forsythe," Miss Sanderson bit off the word. "*Miss* Abigail Sanderson."

"Proctor," the young man gave the secretary a pleasant smile and extended a hand to Forsythe. "David Proctor. And this hasty young lady is Cassandra Dancer."

Forsythe noticed that Sandy had melted and was returning Proctor's smile. The man possessed a sort of dreamy handsomeness. Lush dark hair curled down over his collar and flopped forward over a rounded brow. His brown eyes were soft and warm. Forsythe also noticed the flannel suit

22

was shabby and the collar frayed. Cassandra Dancer wasn't wasting any time on them. She shoved Proctor through the doorway and appeared about to close the door in their faces. "Miss Dancer," he said quickly. "Will you tell Sir Amyas we're here?"

"You tell him. Go around to the rear—"

"Are you sending us to the tradesmen's entrance?" Miss Sanderson asked. Battle flags of color rode high on her cheekbones.

"Of course not. Amy and Carl are mooching around Mandalay. You can't miss it. Just follow the fall of the land." The door closed.

"Well!" Miss Sanderson snapped. "How positively uncouth. We should have rung up Sir Amyas and told him 'no' from London."

"I'm inclined to agree but since we're here we'll tell him in person. On to Mandalay."

His secretary picked her way through the long grass along the side of the house. "Thank God I wore walking shoes. That spoiled brat wouldn't care if we were barefoot. What do you suppose she does that calls for that outlandish getup and David?"

"To say nothing of inspiration. I've no idea but you rhymed David off very quickly. He made an instant hit with you, didn't he?"

"He looks so much like young Lord Byron—that hair, those eyes, that expression."

Smothering a grin, Forsythe gazed around. They were passing the back of the house and could see a good-sized kitchen garden. Farther on a copse straggled down the hill. "You didn't mention servants, Sandy."

"I can see why you mention them. Looks as though there aren't any. There happen to be two. A Mrs. Larkin who is housekeeper and her brother George. Incidentally Willis put a note beside their names. Warned us under no circumstances to refer to them as servants. He didn't say why.

They've been imported because the locals refuse to work for the Dancers." She muttered, "And I damn well can see why."

They entered the wood and beneath the shelter of oak and hemlock branches found a welcome coolness. Forsythe found he was enjoying the exercise and the pure air. Quite a change from the exhaust-laden fumes of London. After a time the trees thinned out and sunlight again beamed down on them. Miss Sanderson paused long enough to slip off her linen jacket and gaze down at the view. "Heavenly," she breathed.

Silently, her companion agreed. The land sloped down to the shores of an ample lake. Willows and alder grew along the banks and directly below them they could see a wooden dock on which could be discerned two men bending over a pile of lumber. Beside the dock a white painted rowboat rode the peaceful water. Directly behind the dock was a structure completely alien to the country scene. If Sir Godfrey Dancer had wanted to reproduce a temple in miniature he had succeeded.

"I adore it," Miss Sanderson said. "It's perfectly enchanting. Look at that red-tile roof, the way it curls up at the edges."

"A charming setting for a murder," Forsythe said laconically and led the way down toward the dock. "What do you think our reception will be?"

"Judging by the daughter of the house I'd say they'll probably toss us off that dock."

This time Miss Sanderson erred in judgment. The older man spotted them first. Throwing down a hammer he strode to meet them. He was short, almost as wide as he was high but it looked like muscle, not fat. Like his daughter's, his face was round but his hair was thinning. A long lock that looked as though it was ordinarily brushed across a bald spot stood out at right angles from his head. His attire was simple and made Forsythe think irrepressibly of Dancer's career as a nudist. All he wore were stout boots and a pair of knee-length khaki shorts that looked like those worn by tropic-zone policemen. The skin over his nose, his arms, and chest was pinkened with what by nightfall would be a bad burn. By the time he reached them his hand was outstretched and he was talking. "Mr. Forsythe and Miss Sanderson, delighted to meet you. Willis said you'd be down today. So good of you to take the trouble. Carleton, come and meet these people."

Carleton came at a lope. He was a head taller than his father and had a reedy build. He had a dark tan and most of it showed. All he wore were slashed-off jeans and desert boots. He was a great deal more hirsute than his sire. A mane of light brown hair fell to his shoulders and his lower face was partially masked by a beard. The beard wasn't a success. It was thin and scraggly.

"Hi," Carleton said, bobbed his head at Miss Sanderson, and gave Forsythe a sweaty hand.

"Doing a little repair work?" Forsythe asked.

Sir Amyas' face became even pinker. "Be doing more than this if it wasn't for those stupid police. Have a look at this." He led them around to the front of the temple and pointed at the brass-covered door. Above an antique padlock was a large red seal. "Damn fools have done everything there is to be done in there. Practically pulled the place to pieces. Even wanted to open Sir Godfrey's tomb. Put my foot down. Told them they'd desecrate my dead over *my* dead body. Phoned Roland—Lord Wabbersley, the chief constable—and he backed me up."

"The body was discovered about two weeks ago, wasn't it?" Forsythe asked. Out of the corner of his eye he noticed Sandy was fishing in her handbag. Turning on the tape machine, he guessed, force of habit.

"About that," the baronet told him wrathfully. "Rang up Roland this morning and he promised a lad would be out to take that ruddy great seal off."

25

"There's not that much hurry, father," his son told him. His voice matched his frame, light, high, reedy.

"Of course there's a hurry. When I get an idea I like to carry it through." Sir Amyas looked around. "Where can we talk? There's a bench over there under that willow. Come along."

Miss Sanderson and Forsythe trailed along after the Dancers. In the shade of the willow was a splintery wooden bench. Dragging a grimy handkerchief from his pocket Sir Amyas spread it on the bench and gallantly seated Miss Sanderson. Forsythe sank down beside her and father and son promptly dropped onto the grass at their feet.

"Suppose you'll want to ask questions," Sir Amyas said. "Fire away."

"Well, my secretary and I do know the details but . . ."

"Bare bones, eh? Want some flesh put on them." The baronet prodded his son's angular shoulder. "You better begin. You're the one responsible for this whole mess."

"I am *not*. I merely brought the girl home. You're the one who offered her a job."

"And I wouldn't have offered her a job if you hadn't sneaked her into the house. What's more—"

"I think," Forsythe said hastily, "it would be simpler if Mr. Dancer—"

"Carleton. Might's well call me that. Everyone does."

"—if Carleton told his story first."

"Not much to tell." The boy's scanty beard bobbed up and down and came to rest on his narrow chest. Both hands were busily engaged in uprooting grass and he looked down at them as he spoke. "I picked her up on the other side of Harper one night about four months ago. Brought her home and the next morning father—"

"Details," Forsythe said patiently.

With much prompting the story was dragged from him. It seemed the younger Dancer had been attending an auction in Chester and was driving back to the Priory when he first

26

saw Katherine St. Croix. "Buttons," he explained. "First Thursday in every month they have a dandy auction in Chester. Pick up some marvelous buttons there. You must see my collection. I hate to brag but it's the finest—"

"Will you forget those stupid buttons?" his father roared. "Get on with it."

"Mr. Forsythe did say he wants full details, father."

"You were driving home," Forsythe prompted.

"It was a bad night. One of those early April nights, cold and slashing rain. Visibility was poor and I was driving slowly and I suppose I might not have noticed her. She was standing by the side of the road, not thumbing, just standing there. I could see her hair blowing in the wind and she had a shoulder bag and this carryall at her feet. It was late, after midnight, and I couldn't figure what a kid like that was doing—"

"She wasn't a kid," his father grunted. "Turned out she was a helluva lot older than you."

"She didn't look it. You figured she was a kid too. In the light from the headlights she looked about eighteen. I stopped the car and asked if she wanted a lift. Told her I could take her into Harper. She said she might as well walk because she had no money to take a room anyway. She was kind of weaving around and I asked whether she was sick. She told me no, she was just lightheaded because she hadn't eaten in a couple of days. I jumped out and persuaded her to get into the car. When I turned on the interior light I could see how wet and forlorn she looked—like a drowned kitten."

"Pretty too," his father said in a milder voice. "A pretty little piece. Fantastic figure but she didn't seem to realize it. Face was so innocent and she had this modest, timid manner. Must admit she took me in too."

"Took us all in," his son admitted gloomily. "Where was I?"

"You put her in the car," Miss Sanderson prompted.

27

"Asked her some questions and she told me she was an orphan, no one to look to for help. Katherine said she'd lost her job at the library in Chester and run out of money to pay her rent. Landlady had slung her out and she was trying to get to London to find work. I couldn't boot her out in that rain so I brought her home. Everyone was bedded down so we went to the kitchen and I got some food into her. She argued all the time, about not wanting to bother me, and what would my family think. Ended up she agreed to spend the night so I made up one of the guest rooms for her and she bedded down. The next morning—" Breaking off, he glared at his father. "You can take it from there."

"Not yet. You left out the buttons."

"So I did. In the kitchen Katherine took off her anorak and under it she had a blouse with five buttons on it. I must admit they riveted my eyes. They were pieces of bone carved into little skulls. I asked her about them and she told me her father had been in Germany at the end of the Second World War and had picked them up. Katherine said he told her they were carved by a guard in a concentration camp and were made from human bone. I . . . I coveted them. I offered to buy them on the spot but she said no, they were all she had left to remember her dad. She had tears in her eyes when she said it. If you want to see them, Mr. Forsythe, I've added them to my collection. As it turned out she lied about them too. Had them checked and they're carved from the bones of a sheep, interesting though."

Forsythe nodded. "You bought these buttons from Miss St. Croix."

"The morning of the day she left . . . at least the day we thought she'd left."

Forsythe's eyes and Miss Sanderson's handbag turned towards the older Dancer. Sir Amyas was vainly trying to pat the long lock across the bald spot. "While I was breakfasting she came down. The rain had stopped and sunlight was beaming into the morning room. She looked as fresh and lovely as a daisy. Katherine told me how kind my son had been and that she wasn't going to infringe on our generosity. She was ready to leave. Had her shoulder bag and her carryall with her. I insisted she have breakfast and she ate ravenously. We talked and she told me the same story she'd told Carleton. I must admit it touched my heart-strings. I'd been thinking of having the family history written and privately printed and when I heard she'd worked in a library—"

"Crap!" His son said inelegantly. "You'd never even considered it."

Sir Amyas rubbed his round chin. "I'll be truthful. It hadn't occurred to me. But I did want her to stay on. She was too proud to accept money without working and she was so young and such a stunner I figured some cad would take advantage of—"

Carleton glared at his father. "You figured you might as well keep her here and take advantage of her yourself."

His glare was returned and Forsythe looked from one man to the other. Neither had much claim to good looks but shared wonderfully shaped, high-bridged noses. Too bad, he thought, Cassandra hadn't inherited a nose like theirs instead of her small snout. He asked the men, "Could you stick to the facts?"

Sir Amyas took a deep and apparently calming breath. "Correct. Katherine made asses of us all. With the exception of Mrs. Larkin and my daughter. They saw through her immediately." He broke off a long blade of grass and nibbled at the end. "After much persuading Katherine agreed to stay on and research and write the book. I set up the library for her and she went to work. She seemed so . . . so sincere and serious about it. I provided her with all the old records, the diaries, and every time I saw the girl she had a sheaf of notes or a book. With my permission she interviewed the rest of the family, my father-in-law and my sisters. She even went to Harper to see young Proctor—"

"Is David Proctor a relative?" Forsythe inquired.

"No, but we regard the lad as family. David was a protégé of my late wife. He's a poet and completely unworldly. Viola insisted Proctor leave London and come down here and I feel rather responsible for him. His only sources of income are from music lessons and an occasional poem he has published. Right now he's playing for my daughter while she—" He turned to his son "Exactly *what* is Cassandra doing?"

Carleton shrugged a leather-brown shoulder. "Haven't the foggiest."

"Anyway, whatever Cassandra is doing, young Proctor is helping her."

"How long was Miss St. Croix with you?" Forsythe asked.

Sir Amyas looked baffled. "Never keep track of time. Eight . . . maybe nine days."

"Ten," Miss Sanderson said crisply. "Carleton picked her up in the early hours of Friday morning and she disappeared a week from the following Sunday."

"That's right. Funny, it seems much longer. Must admit I took a fancy to the girl and spent a lot of time with her. Told her all about the family and she seemed interested. Wonderful listener, Katherine was."

Forsythe regarded the Dancer father and son. The baronet was nibbling on a fresh spear of grass and Carleton still seemed intent on uprooting the rest. "Neither of you had any hint she was thinking of leaving?"

Sir Amyas removed the strand of grass and gazed down at it. "Only time I saw her that Sunday was at breakfast time. She seemed the same as usual, quiet and demure. Of course, Cassandra never let on to anyone about what she'd found out and she didn't speak to Katherine until mid-morning."

"You didn't see Miss St. Croix for the rest of the day?"

"At lunchtime she sent George down with a message. Said she wasn't feeling well and was going to rest."

Carleton looked up. "I saw her. Three times. At the breakfast table and later in the morning. Not sure of the time. It was before lunch. Maybe about eleven-thirty. She came to my room and asked whether I was still interested in buying her buttons. Told her yes and we haggled on price a bit. Finally settled on ten pounds per, so I went down to father and he got fifty pounds out of the safe. All small bills so I stuck an elastic band around them. I took them up to her room and she opened the door, handed me the buttons, and took the money. Said she had a headache and was going to rest. That was the last I saw of her."

Miss Sanderson said. "I understand you never keep money anywhere but in the safe."

"Not now," Sir Amyas told her. "Used to have it lying around in drawers but last year our London house was burgled and we lost money, a few bits of jewelry, and some silver. Since then Cassandra insists we keep the valuables in our bank and only a small amount of cash in the safe. Sensible girl, Cassandra." He rubbed the sunburned tip of his shapely nose. "Terrible shock the next morning when Mrs. Larkin told us Katherine was gone and her baggage, such as it was, with her. Couldn't believe she'd leave like that."

"Your daughter didn't let on to you about the reason for Miss St. Croix's hasty departure?"

"Didn't even peep about it until her body was found and then Cassandra had to tell the police. Couldn't believe that, either. A common crook!"

Rather an uncommon one, Forsythe thought, able to inveigle her way into the Dancer house and enthrall not only Carleton but his father. Sir Amyas was still rambling on about the shock and his son was staring into space. Better check the time span, the barrister thought, and turned not to the two men but to Miss Sanderson. His secretary told him crisply, "Sir Amyas discovered the body three months and ten days from the time she arrived here."

Sir Amyas gave her a beaming smile. "Wish you worked for me, Miss Sanderson. Got a good mind."

"Fifteen days ago," Forsythe mused. "How did you happen to enter the temple, Sir Amyas?"

Miss Sanderson leaned forward. "And weren't you afraid to?"

"Afraid?" Sir Amyas rolled the word around on his tongue, as though tasting it.

"The runes. The curse."

"Oh, that. No, that's only for defiling the place. And I shouldn't think it would apply to Dancers."

His son gave him a sidelong glance. "Should think uprooting Sir Godfrey's ancient bones would be defiling it."

"Only to move them to our burial plot at St. Jude, son. Nothing wrong with that. Planning to give Godfrey a little service too." Sir Amyas swung his head back toward Forsythe. "First time I'd ever been inside Mandalay. Maybe the first time anyone has been since Cuthbert locked it up. Except for Katherine, of course."

"I understand that there's only one key for the padlock?"

"Whacking great thing. Always been kept in the drawer of a table in the entrance hall. Had to root through a mess of junk to find it. Wondered afterwards how Katherine laid her hands on it."

"You told her," his son muttered. "I heard you, when you were raving on about Mandalay and Sir Godfrey."

"Don't recall that. Anyone could have told her. No secret where the key was kept."

Forsythe shifted on the bench. "Your reason for entering the temple?"

"Wanted to look around and see whether there were materials there I could use in the Roman amphitheater."

Forsythe and his secretary spoke like a Greek chorus. "Amphitheater?"

In the midst of the scraggly beard Carleton's full lips turned up into a broad grin. "Father's going to pull down Mandalay and put up a Roman amphitheater."

"Not the full oval," Sir Amyas confided. "Just a chunk of one like this." His hands formed a slice shaped like a piece of pie.

Carleton was convulsed with laughter. "Better change the name of the lake, father. How about the Adriatic Sea?"

Sir Amyas' round face, which had been getting steadily redder, now was purple. "You perfect ass! Making fun of a fine idea! You've got a lot to talk about. Not long ago you were on stage swinging your hips and tossing out legs and arms to a bunch of young twits!"

His son sobered and said sulkily, "It was a gimmick, father. Rock bands have to have gimmicks."

"Ghoulish one. Didn't like it at all. Didn't like it when you pelted the audience with severed heads for a finale either. Glad you had to give it up."

Having squelched his son, Sir Amyas turned his attention back to Forsythe and his secretary. Hastily, Miss Sanderson asked, "What will you *use* it for?"

"Use?" The baronet paused apparently to savor this word too. "Aesthetic value. There's an amphitheater at Chester. People come in droves to see it."

Carleton entered the fray again. "Wouldn't put it past father to throw it open to the public and charge admission."

"Day trippers on my property? No, son, this is for the family's use."

Miss Sanderson was fascinated. "But what *use*, Sir Amyas?"

He pondered and then said, "Musical evenings. We could make up our own group. Carleton plays an electric guitar and Proctor's good on the piano. I play the drums or

33

did at one time. Cassandra—what instrument did she take lessons on, Carleton?"

"Think it was the harp. Hey, this isn't a bad idea, father. Mrs. Larkin sings rather well and so does George. Have to find a gimmick."

"No gimmicks, son. No legs or arms or heads."

While the Dancers argued about gimmicks Forsythe shook a baffled head. Vainly he tried to picture an electric guitar, drums, and a harp pumping music from a Roman amphitheater out over the placid lake. Miss Sanderson muttered in his ear, "Think we'd better get out of here. Whatever they have is contagious. This whole business is starting to sound logical, Robby."

Forsythe broke into the argument. "I think we'd better get back to the discovery of Miss St. Croix's body."

"Righto," Sir Amyas said. "When I got the temple unlocked I found a couple of candles standing in their own wax on top of Sir Godfrey's tomb. Turned out Katherine had taken them from the dining room. There's no electricity laid on in the temple so I'd brought a torch. Shone it around and caught sight of the glass cabinet where the jade statuettes were kept. They'd been sealed in and now the glass had been smashed and the two pink ones were missing. I lit the candles and started looking around. Figured at first some vandals had managed to get in. Then my foot touched something on the floor and I looked down and saw Katherine's carryall with the top gaping open. Looked further and found her shoulder bag against the wall."

"You recognized both of them?"

"Not the carryall—plastic affair with a zipper and a couple of carrying straps. Cheap. Could have been anyone's. But the bag was distinctive—big and kind of homespun material with a pattern of red and yellow and orange, not stripes, kind of zigzags. Primitive. Could be Mayan—"

"Aztec," Carleton corrected.

"Took a closer look and found brown splotches all over the floor around the carryall. I finally decided they looked like blood and I got alarmed. Then I saw the metal bar. Flat end of it had stuff encrusted on it. Caught hell from the police afterward for using it—"

"Was this bar kept in the temple?"

"Must have been. The police had it examined and it's old. It might have been left after Sir Godfrey was stuck in the tomb." Sir Amyas paused and looked down at his hands. He looked suddenly older and sick. "I picked up the bar and slid it under the top of the empty tomb. It took a little doing but I got it open and the smell was awful. She'd been crammed down into it and . . ." His mouth worked. "Don't care if Katherine was a crook; that's a hideous way for a woman to die. Back of her head battered in." He covered his face with his hands. "God!"

His son awkwardly patted the bowed shoulders. "Father was shattered and so was I. We'd just been getting used to the idea she'd left without a word, and then that."

Forsythe addressed himself to the younger man. "The police found some interesting things in her carryall, didn't they?"

"The two statuettes were wrapped up in her clothes and there was money. The money was near the top and had been splattered by blood and . . . other things. From her head, you know. There were two lots of notes. One was the fifty pounds I'd given her for the buttons. I had no trouble identifying them. The elastic band I put around them came from ones I use for boxes of buttons. Wide pink affairs. The other bundle of notes had an ordinary thin band around it. There was a hundred pounds in that one."

"Miss St. Croix couldn't have stolen that hundred pounds from any of you?"

Carleton's shaggy head shook. "Our money is in father's safe and none was missing. The aunts never have much cash around their house and Grandfather Gillimede doesn't have money. Hates it. No, Katherine didn't steal it from us."

Miss Sanderson was thoughtfully nibbling her lower lip. "The police think the victim was on her knees beside the carryall, perhaps putting the second piece of jade into it, when she was struck on the back of the head. The murderer didn't leave a trace. Just smudges on the top of the tombs. They think the killer was wearing gloves. They also say the jade is incredibly valuable. Why on earth was it left in the temple?"

"It has always been there," Carleton said earnestly. "We never thought of it in terms of value. It was simply part of Sir Godfrey's mausoleum."

Forsythe bent forward. "Have either of you any idea of the identity of the murderer?"

Sir Amyas' hands fell away from his face. "Some villian must have killed her. When the police brought in that young fellow who'd helped her dispose of some of the things she stole . . . what was his name?"

"Fred Small," Miss Sanderson said. "Alias Scoppy Smaile. He has a record of petty crime and did work with the murdered woman on occasion. But he has an alibi. At the time of her death Scoppy was in jail for drunken driving."

Carleton straightened and said, "I think it's someone from Katherine's past. She ripped off a lot of people, you know. Got herself into their homes and took everything that wasn't nailed down. Like Aunt Pru Pyne in Harper. Katherine did her a few months before she had a go at us."

Forsythe cocked his head. "You feel one of the people she victimized followed her here and killed her?"

"Well, if she'd had a falling out with a confederate I think he'd have taken the money and the jade. Looks to me as though it was revenge."

Carleton Dancer might be a bit odd, Forsythe thought, but there was nothing wrong with his reasoning. When his father spoke it was apparent a certain amount of clear thinking did run through the family. "Wrong, son. I'd like to think that but there are a couple of things wrong with that solution. How did this avenger know Katherine would be in the temple? And how on earth did a stranger know where to put the key back? It was returned to the table in the hall, you know. Has to be someone connected with the family, someone who knew where the key was kept."

"If you hadn't gotten that idea about pulling Mandalay down, father, this mess would never have happened. The body could have been in there for a hundred years and no one would have been the wiser."

"And if you hadn't dragged the girl here in the first place, son, she'd still be alive." Sir Amyas added, "That's all we know, Mr. Forsythe. The police are stymied and I'm banking on you to clear this up."

Time, Forsythe thought. He stood up and nodded at Miss Sanderson. Her hand crept into her handbag to turn off the tape recorder. Their two companions pulled themselves up, the younger man lithely, Sir Amyas with more effort. The baronet, even half-naked, sunburned, and with the lock of hair sticking waggishly out from his head, had a kind of dignity. Before the barrister could speak, he held up a silencing hand. "I know what you're going to say, Mr. Forsythe. You're going to tell us you won't take the case. You're going to tell us the police have much better facilities than you have to get to the bottom of it."

"Yes. And I was about to suggest a professional private investigator. Sir Amyas, I'm truly sorry."

"I'm sorry too. Sorry you don't understand our position. I thought you would. That was one reason I asked Willis Seton to talk with you. You must realize, Mr. Forsythe, that the police have no evidence to charge any of us. You must also realize they have no evidence to *clear* any of us." The baronet held Forsythe's eyes. "I happen to know a good deal about your own past. Not from Willis, from other sources. Some years ago you were under a cloud yourself. You cleared your professional reputation but you must know how we feel. Friends turning away from you, papers printing personal details that are almost, but not quite, libelous. If the person who murdered Katherine St. Croix isn't exposed this will get worse with time. The public will forget she was a petty crook. They'll think of her as an innocent young girl who was lured to this estate and foully murdered by a mad Dancer."

Sir Amyas paused for breath and then asked quietly, "How did *you* feel when a veil of suspicion hung over your life?"

"Like a pariah," Forsythe said bluntly.

"And that's how we feel but in our case there's little chance of reprieve. Mr. Forsythe, I'm imploring you to at least try."

"If I agree I must warn you that the murderer I uncover may be a member of your family. Perhaps it will be you."

Carleton leaped forward. "Father *found* the body. He's the one who insisted on calling *you* in. Would he do that if he'd killed Katherine?"

"What better way to avert suspicion from himself?" Forsythe asked evenly.

Sir Amyas put a restraining hand on his son's arm. "I'll take that chance. If one of my household is guilty I want him or her punished. It's terrible to even contemplate, but the innocent shouldn't suffer for the rest of their lives. Find the person who killed Katherine, no matter who it is."

The barrister took a deep breath. "Very well. I'll take the case."

Wiping a hand down his khaki shorts, Sir Amyas extended it and Forsythe solemnly shook it. The bargain was sealed.

CHAPTER FOUR

IN THE WOODS ABOVE THE CHINA SEA FORSYTHE LEANED against the bole of an oak and watched Miss Sanderson deftly inserting a fresh tape into her little machine. As she closed the flap of her handbag he said, "Let the other shoe drop, Sandy. I can't stand the suspense." She lifted a brow and he added, "Make some remark about turning Sir Amyas down kindly but firmly."

"No comment."

"Why not?"

"When he dragged up our past, there was no other answer you could give him. That Dancer may be bizarre but he's bright enough."

"Perhaps bright enough to get away with murder."

She tucked her bag under an arm and linked her other arm with his. "Where away?"

"To interview another member of the household. Anyone we can get our hands on."

When they reached the kitchen garden they found a man stooping over the long rows of vegetables. He straightened and stared but said nothing. He looked about forty and wore dark trousers and an immaculate white jacket. His most outstanding feature was his neck—long, thin, serpentine. The bulge of an Adam's apple in that stringy throat reminded Forsythe unpleasantly of a mouse being slowly digested by a snake.

"That has to be George," Miss Sanderson muttered.

"Strong silent type."

"Silent, anyway." They rounded the house and Miss Sanderson pointed. "Looks like we're in luck. Cassandra is waving goodbye to David Proctor."

They glanced from the figure hunched over the handlebars of the ancient bike to the girl standing on the top step, shielding her eyes against the sun. Cassandra was still wearing her scanty costume but had added a sweatband over her hair. As she turned toward the door she caught sight of them. "Hello, again."

They mounted the steps and Forsythe asked, "Could you spare a few moments?"

"I suppose so. David tells me I was madly rude to you earlier."

"You were," Miss Sanderson told her.

"Sorry. I get so worked up when the inspiration arrives and David doesn't. Do come in and grill me all you wish."

Forsythe raised his brows. "You know why we're here then?"

"Amy told all of us and warned we'd better cooperate. I'll give you a guided tour before I tell all." She pointed at a long table standing against the wall in the entrance hall. "The fatal key is, or rather was, kept in that drawer. Right now the police have it and Amy, poor darling, is raising hell about it."

The table was cluttered. Among other objects Forsythe noticed an unstrung tennis racket, a number nine iron, a motorcycle helmet, a pair of driving gloves, and a half-eaten candy bar. The drawer the girl pulled out was filled with odds and ends, balls of twine, envelopes, a broken cigarette case. Cassandra ran a fingertip along the surface of the table and left a mark. "This house is a mess," she said.

From what Forsythe could see he was inclined to agree. The tiled floor was grubby and the noble staircase undusted. A picture hung crookedly over the table. Cassandra, talking steadily, led the way up that noble dusty staircase. "When mother was alive it was different. Of course the aunts were still with us and Aunt Sybil is one person who can get some work out of the Lark. And Aunt Bella is worth about six housemaids."

"You do have a couple of servants," Miss Sanderson pointed out.

"For heaven's sake, don't let the Lark hear you say that." Cassandra reached the landing, took a sharp right turn, and continued to lead the way steadily upward. "According to her, George and she are distant connections of the Dancers and they're 'helping out.' The Lark also prides herself on 'standing by us in our time of need.' The truth is that you couldn't pry her loose. Has her heart set on being the next Lady Dancer."

"How long has she been with you?" Forsythe asked.

"Five . . . no, about six years."

Miss Sanderson was starting to pant. The third set of stairs were even steeper and Cassandra set a rapid pace. The secretary had been clinging to the bannister and she examined the coating of dust she'd picked up on her palm. "Don't you have cleaners?"

"We did until the news leaked out about Katherine jammed in that crypt. I offered the cleaners double salary but they ran for cover, fearing for their lives. That ruddy woman is more trouble dead than she was alive and that's saying something."

"How much farther?" Forsythe gasped.

"One flight. At the end of this hall." Cassandra looked back. "You're out of shape. Should do some exercises." She led the way down a long corridor floored with faded

41

carpet and lithely started climbing a structure much like a ladder.

"Do you live on the roof?" Miss Sanderson groaned.

"In the attic. Artists should always live in garrets, don't you think?"

Miss Sanderson hauled herself up through a trapdoor and sank onto the first chair she reached, a straight-backed wooden affair. Thankfully, Forsythe lowered himself on the only other chair and looked around. The room was huge, bare, and spotlessly clean. On uneven planking an exercise mat was stretched, and the far wall was covered with a mirror, a bar running its length. Against the other wall was an upright piano with yellowing keys. Cassandra took up a position in front of the mirror and put a hand on the brass bar. She wasn't breathing heavily. "Pretty nice, isn't it? I had it fixed up when I came home from the States. Bedroom and bath through there. Think I'll have a sauna installed. Dancing is such sweaty work."

"Ballet?" Miss Sanderson asked.

"Started out that way. I studied ballet for a time and then found it wasn't . . . I suppose you'd say expressive enough for me. David and I are working on dancing that is complete self-expression. A terrible grind and takes so much time but he says sacrifice is essential for a true artist. Mind if I do a few exercises while we talk?"

"Not at all." Forsythe leaned back in his chair, watching one trim leg lever itself up over the bar. Cassandra definitely had a good build.

"You'll want to hear all about the wicked witch of the west."

"In time. Perhaps you could fill in your background first."

"Where would you like me to start? The Crusades or the Magna Carta?"

"With your mother, I think."

Cassandra executed a pirouette and raised the other leg.

"She's dead. Died almost a year ago—on her birthday. I think I'd better be totally honest with you. Most of my earlier life was spent at boarding schools and I didn't know mother all that well. What I did know about her I didn't like. Her death was a shock, but I'm not a hypocrite and I won't pretend a grief I don't feel."

Miss Sanderson looked faintly taken aback. "What didn't you like about her?"

"She had a terrible strength—the strength of the weak. I'm not very good with words but she was like a . . . vine. Wrapped herself around one and choked out the life."

"An ivy and an oak?" Forsythe murmured.

"Similar. Mother was fragile and kind of droopy and very decorative. She didn't have any luck with me and Amy is not the kind to be choked but she did one hell of a job on Carl. He was only about three when Amy and mother were married and she devoured him. Carl deludes himself about adoring her but deep down I think he disliked her as much as I did." Deserting the bar, Cassandra fell gracefully on the mat and proceeded to do pushups. Her skin was glossy with sweat and she spoke in jerks. "From as far back as I can remember Amy was angling for divorce. He gave mother every excuse to get one. Amy's a great man for the ladies, particularly young ones, and he's had a succession of totties he's kept in Chester and London. He really was quite blatant about his girls but mother didn't turn a hair. In turn she had a succession of protégés. All young and male and good-looking. Her way of fighting back, I guess."

"Physical affairs?" Forsythe asked.

"If you mean did she sleep with them—no. Not her way. These were unions of the mind and spirit—soulful . . . sonnets and such, looking deep into eyes and sighing. I remember a few of them. The curate of St. Jude was an early one. Dabbled in painting and did rather horrible little watercolors." The girl rolled over on her back and looked up at the rafters. Her breasts, Forsythe noticed with some

43

satisfaction, were heaving. She giggled. "Must tell you about Alec. Mother had become interested in rehabilitation. Took young, always artistic, and nice-looking men from places like clinics and mental institutions and brought them here for weekends. None of them gave us any trouble until she came up with Alec. Alec was definitely a horse of another color. Mother never provided any details on their pasts and I don't think she really knew much about them herself. Went strictly by soulful eyes and nice features. Alec was a handsome brute, dark and swarthy and madly sexy. He also, as we found out, had tried to poison his entire family. The weekend he came the Lark served fresh strawberries for dessert and we were all spooning sugar on them like crazy. They tasted a little gritty but we licked the bowls clean and then Alec looked soulfully up and told us he'd mixed arsenic with the sugar."

"Blimey," Miss Sanderson whispered.

Cassandra groaned and pulled herself into a sitting position. She massaged one calf. "Cramp. That hurts. How one must suffer for art! Ah, better. Where was I? Oh, Alec and arsenic. We bolted from the table and every w.c. in the house was filled with people forcing their fingers down their throats and upchucking. Amy couldn't find an unoccupied one and bent over the sink in the scullery. That was the end not only of Alec but of mother's charity work; Amy and Uncle Roly put down their feet."

"Arsenic," Miss Sanderson said faintly.

"Uncle Roly?" Forsythe asked.

Cassandra's close-set eyes turned to him. "It wasn't poison. Alec couldn't come up with any on the spot, thank God, so he settled for fruit salts. Uncle Roly is not an uncle. He's my godfather. He's chief constable and comes in handy." She settled gracefully and effortlessly into a full lotus.

In that position, Forsythe thought, with her body gleaming with sweat, she looks like a metal statue. Except for the round plain face, of course. Pity that face didn't live up to the body's promise. "David Proctor was Lady Dancer's last protégé?"

"The last and the best. Mother met him at some do in London and persuaded him to give up his little job, come to Harper, and devote all his time to writing. He's a wonderful writer, sensitive and talented. But he's working in the wrong area. Poetry isn't really for him. He'd do much better writing novels." Her expression was dreamy and she looked into space. "This is my time to meditate. The sacrifices I make for Amy."

"As well as for art," Miss Sanderson said tartly. Lowering her voice she muttered, "Three guesses about the handsome genius she meditates about."

"Your father," Forsythe prompted. "How did he feel about his wife's protégés?"

"Ecstatic. Always hoping his Viola would fall madly in love and run off and leave him. When David hove into view Amy was delighted. Practically chucked the old girl into David's arms. Offered mother a handsome settlement if she would up and divorce him."

"Why didn't *he* divorce her?"

A gleaming shoulder moved in a shrug. "A number of reasons. His Viola was clever enough not to give him grounds. And Dancers never divorce. The aunts are dead set against divorce. I really think Aunt Sybil would rather that a relative knock off an unwanted spouse than divorce. And to give Amy his due, he's a gentleman. Let his name be sullied, not his wife's. As for mother . . . she seemed so easily swayed but I noticed she never did anything she didn't want to. Prattled on about duty. How she *loved* using that word. Duty to stay with her children even if her husband was a beast, duty to her dear old dad, who is even loonier about divorce than the aunts. Duty! She stayed because she *liked* being Lady Dancer, *liked* being considered a martyr. But she really fell for David and it looked as though she was going to forget duty and devote her life to him. Then her birthday arrived and she drowned."

"Do you mind telling us about her death?" Forsythe asked.

"No, but I fail to see what bearing this has on Katherine the crook."

"One never knows. Anyway, it does help fill in the family relationships."

"I suppose so." Cassandra looked dubious but continued, "On the first day of August we had a bit of a birthday bash for mother. Even Gramps came and he seldom sets foot in this house. Considers it a mixture of Sodom, Gomorrah, and a sporting house. He was invited for dinner but he didn't eat. Among other things he's sort of a vegetarian. Lives off the land, he boasts. What Gramps does is sneak into our kitchen garden and the aunts' in the dark of night and swipes vegetables. He could have all he wants any old time but he prefers snitching them. Gramps is a bit loony, you know."

"As well as everyone else in the family," Miss Sanderson muttered.

If Cassandra heard that remark she didn't let on. "Let's see, there were mother and Amy and Carl and me. The aunts weren't there. They decamped after Aunt Sybil had a blazing row with Amy about a fortnight before. Took up residence in the Dower House. Anyway, Gramps arrived all tarted up in a new toga and had made a crown of oak leaves for his hair. He—"

"Neither your aunts nor grandfather live in the house?"

"As I said the aunts are living in the Dower House. I miss them. They're old pussies and Aunt Bella is a wonderful cook. The Lark handles that now and she dishes up some unbelievable messes for meals. If she's trying to become Lady Dancer she's wasting her time. No one can get to Amy through his stomach anyway. Luckily he could eat boiled shoe leather and not notice it. No, the Lark will have to use sex. She's not a bad-looking woman for her age."

"How old is Mrs. Larkin?"

"About thirty-five. Too old for Amy. You'll loathe her. She's so *genteel*. You've got me confused. What did you want to know?"

"Your Grandfather Gillimede—his quarters."

"He's lived for years in the ruins of the Priory, a rubble of stones on the other side of the woods. Incidentally, when you interview him don't let him tempt you into his lair. Both Gramps and his quarters smell like old goat. I told him that cleanliness is next to godliness but he countered that he's mortifying the flesh and feeding the soul. But he's quite harmless and rather a dear. To get back to the birthday bash, Gramps arrived in his weird costume but this time mother had done him one better. Usually she lounged around in filmy romantic dresses but when she came down for dinner she was dressed as a sailor—"

"You're joking." Miss Sanderson massaged her temples.

"Not at all. She'd had the outfit made up on the sly and sprang it on us that night. All white and red and blue, middy blouse, bell-bottomed pants, even a little sailor hat. Amy seldom notices anything but he noticed *that*." Cassandra smiled but there was a touch of sadness in the smile. "David was the unwitting reason for the outfit and I suppose, in a way, for her death. They both, mother and David, had this terrible fear of water. Between the sonnets and the soul-searching glances they'd decided they should overcome this weakness. So, mother put on her sailor suit and later that night without telling a soul went down to the China Sea and got into the boat there. It overturned and . . ." Cassandra's voice trailed off. "Sorry, but it was rather a beastly way for a person terrified of water to die. Mother wasn't missed until the following morning. I rang up David and he came out from Harper and we all searched. We went through the woods and around the Dower House

47

and the Priory ruins and—Gramps was the only one who went to the lake—we didn't think she'd be near water. He shouted and when we got down there we found the rowboat overturned and adrift and her little white hat floating on the water. Carl was the one who pulled her out . . ."

"Don't continue," Forsythe told the girl gently. "I'm sorry to distress you."

Cassandra unfolded and came to her feet. She began touching her toes. "The most distressing part of it is that except for Gramps and David, none of us really cared that much. Oh, we were stunned for a time but we didn't love her. They did. Carl seemed shattered but, as I said, I think he was subconsciously relieved. Mother really was a trial."

"Now we will move on to Katherine St. Croix," the barrister said. "Your father said you and Mrs. Larkin distrusted her from the time she arrived."

"I think the Lark distrusted Katherine more as competition than anything else."

Miss Sanderson shifted on the hard seat. "What was Miss St. Croix like?"

"A stunner—fantastic figure." The girl straightened and her hands described airy lush curves over her more modest ones. "She had a face like a madonna, oval, with huge brown eyes and long dark lashes. She had a mass of light hair, bleached, but it was a splendid job, no dark roots. But it wasn't her looks that were dangerous; it was the way she used them. Had a habit of casting her eyes down, so modestly, and shoving out her—like this." Cassandra lowered her chin slightly and looked down so her straw-colored lashes hid her eyes. At the same time she arched her back, bringing her breasts jutting against the pink bikini top. "Touch me, touch me not, if you know what I mean. Such a modest, innocent stick of dynamite. I took one look at her and thought, you'll bear watching, my girl."

"What was her manner to you?" Forsythe asked.

"Same act she used on the others, smarmy and ingratiating. Kept telling us she was too much trouble, she didn't want to impose. In the meantime she was raising hell. She had Amy and Carl at each other's throats and even George was trailing along after her with his tongue lolling out. When she went to the ruins to interview Gramps I was hoping he'd give her short shrift. Thought he'd take one look and decide she was a sinner from hell. Odd thing is that's exactly the line she took with him. Had him convinced she was repentant and he could save her soul. Katherine must have thoroughly researched the family before she wormed her way into the house." Cassandra chuckled. "She had no luck with the aunts. Aunt Sybil saw through her immediately and told her to get out and stay out."

"And you distrusted her and took steps to stop her?"

"I had to. There was no one else." The girl leaned back against the exercise bar. "I watched the havoc she was wreaking. There was no sense in trying to talk to Amy or Carl. Both of them were infatuated with the woman. I could see she had her sights on Amy and was using Carl to push the poor old dear into a proposal. Imagine having Katherine St. Croix as a stepmother! But the bitter end was when she went after David. While she was here David was in and out but she didn't pay much attention to him. Then she went into Harper to see him. David and I had a row over that and he took *her* part. Said I had a filthy mind and the poor kid only wanted advice on how to start her book. *Kid.* Katherine was years older than David."

"That's when you hired a private investigator?" Forsythe asked.

"Katherine went to see David the Monday after she arrived. On Tuesday I hotfooted up to London and picked a name from the telephone directory. Turned out I got a little chap who specialized in divorces. Private investigators are such slimy creatures, aren't they?" She glanced at Miss Sanderson's outraged face and said hastily, "Present com-

49

pany excepted, of course. Anyway, Mr. Forsythe, this work is only your hobby, isn't it?"

"You could call it that," Forsythe said wryly. "What happened then?"

"Nothing much for a couple of days. Katherine strolled around clutching notebooks and rubbing herself against Amy and Carl. George's eyes were swiveling and the Lark was looking pure murder at the woman. Then . . . then the bitch had the audacity to go to Harper and visit David again. That was a Thursday and I felt much like the Lark did. I could have slit the woman's throat!"

"Are you and David engaged?" Miss Sanderson asked.

"As far as I'm concerned we are. David is being difficult. He says it's too soon after mother's death. But he'll come around. All David needs is a firm hand." Cassandra's mouth set in a firm line. "He doesn't realize what a narrow squeak he had. If mother had lived and divorced Amy, David would have married her and she'd have ruined him. Kept him writing those silly poems and dancing attendance on her. Then there was the age difference."

"How old was your mother?" Miss Sanderson asked.

"Forty-two. Not much younger than you. Positively ancient!"

Forsythe cast an apprehensive look at his secretary. Cassandra Dancer had put her foot in her mouth this time. Sandy's weak point was her age. It was her secret and she disliked any reference to it. And if looks could kill Cassandra was now being annihilated. Oblivious to the faux pas, the girl rushed on. "On Friday I rang up my slimy little man and asked whether he had any information on Katherine. He said he had a batch and could mail it to me. I told him I would come up on Saturday and pick it up. The next day I found out David was going to London to see a publisher or agent or something and I thought we could get our business done and make a day of it. But David had too much to do so I drove back by myself. David stayed the night and he had the most incredible hard luck. A hotel thief ripped off his room and got all the little presents mother had given him—a gold cigarette case and pencil set and an expensive watch."

Forsythe raised a brow. "Did your mother, ah, support Mr. Proctor?"

"Not exactly. Mother wasn't all that generous. When she tempted David down to Harper I believe she paid his expenses for a few months but then insisted he give music lessons to take care of his room and board. Oh, she gave him silly useless presents and perhaps a little check now and then but you've seen him. His clothes are a disgrace and he won't take a penny from me. So proud."

Forsythe was wondering why David Proctor had been willing to take everything he could get from the mother and was too proud to take a penny from the daughter. Cassandra was smiling, a tender, wistful smile. "When we're married it will be different. David will have everything he deserves. Carl and I have our own money. Grandfather Dancer didn't quite trust Amy with money so he provided for his grandchildren and his daughters." The smile expanded and became a laugh. "I chatter so much I get right away from what I'm trying to tell you. Back to Katherine and the denouement. I came back from London clutching my ammunition and I must say I was delighted. Katerina Padrinski alias Katherine St. Croix alias Katie Parr had a past that was a beaut.

"Her specialty was much the same as the scam she'd pulled on us. Look over a prosperous family, eel her way into the house, and then steal anything that wasn't nailed down. Sometimes she worked with a male confederate, sometimes she worked alone. When she was stealing she ordinarily handed down the loot to her male friend from her bedroom window. Most of the time she posed as a domestic and with the servant problem had little difficulty getting into houses. Like Aunt Pru's for instance."

"Prudence Pyne," Miss Sanderson told Forsythe tersely. "Harper."

"That's correct," Cassandra said. "Courtesy aunt. She's creaking with age, much older than either of my aunts, but she's close friends with them. Aunt Pru was good with mother too. Let her rave on about her tough life and being pulled two ways, duty versus love. That sort of thing. Everyone talks to Aunt Pru. I do. She has a lovely shoulder to cry on. Anyway, Katherine turned out to be a disgusting crook. There was one thing the investigator dug up that really disturbed me. Katherine took a position as a companion to a very old woman, partially invalided. The woman didn't have much, her cottage was rented and all she had were a few sticks of furniture, a little jewelry, and a small insurance policy. But she willed all of it to Katherine and then she fell downstairs and broke her neck. Her son was convinced Katherine had pushed his mother and he raised a stink, but there was no evidence and no charges were laid."

Forsythe asked, "Did you face Miss St. Croix with this evidence when you returned from London?"

"No. I suppose I took time to gloat. But the next day— Sunday—I asked her to come up here after breakfast, and then handed her the report. She started to read it and went positively livid. Quite honestly, with her mask off the woman was terrifying. She cursed and raved on about everyone in the family. Called Amy a dirty old man and Carl an idiot and . . . on and on. Not in those words. Katherine was a guttersnipe and talked like one."

"Were you afraid of a physical attack?"

"Hardly." Raising an arm, Cassandra flexed a sizable muscle. "It was worse than that. After a time she calmed down and she was even more frightening. Promised if I exposed her she'd swear Carl had held her down and Amy had raped her. Told me she would smear the whole family. Tell the police Gramps had attacked her and he would be put in a looney bin. With her record I knew the police wouldn't

52

take it seriously, but it would be spread all over the yellow sheets and people would believe that filth. They always do, you know.

"That was when I realized I had to use her own tactics on her." Cassandra raised her chin with hauteur and Forsythe could see the centuries of breeding that had produced this girl. Plain or not, she was an aristocrat.

"What did you do?" he asked.

"She knew Uncle Roly—Lord Wabbersley—is my godfather. I told her I'd swear I saw her stealing my pearl necklace and she would go to jail. Katherine was clever and she knew whose word would be taken on something like that. I watched her face change and she went right back to meek, smarmy old Katherine. She started to cry like someone turning on a tap and told me I had no idea what it was like for a girl to have to make her own way. Sobbed about being an orphan and falling in with bad companions. Threw herself on my mercy and told me if I let her stay on she would be able to reform. Katherine was a wonderful actress. For a few moments she had me wavering and then I remembered the old woman who fell to her death. So I made a bargain with her. She agreed to get out of the house and out of our lives. I told her if she was still here on Monday morning I'd go to the chief constable."

Regarding the girl with curiosity, Miss Sanderson asked, "Once you had Miss St. Croix's record why didn't you take it to your father and brother?"

"You'd have to know them better to understand, Miss Sanderson. Amy and Carl have to be . . . they have to be protected. They're mere babes; have their own little worlds and seldom touch reality. I couldn't have them faced with this dirty business."

"So," the barrister drawled. "On Monday morning when you found Miss St. Croix was gone you thought she had fulfilled her end of your bargain."

"Yes and I was delighted. I thought that was the end of

her. Carl and Amy wandered around like lost souls but I knew they would get over it. They're both resilient. I comforted them by saying Katherine was probably a rover and had just gotten bored and left. Time passed and they both bounced back. Then—" The girl's body sagged with dejection. "Amy had to get that idea about turning Mandalay into an amphitheater and discovered the bloody body. The police swarmed in, just about drove us mad, and didn't come up with a solid lead. The papers are raving on about those decadent Dancers and—oh hell!"

"Yes," Forsythe agreed, "an uncomfortable position for you and your family. Could you tell us about the Sunday night that Miss St. Croix was murdered?"

The girl sank down on the exercise mat. "I'm tired of the whole business. But you are trying to help and Amy says you're our only hope of clearing this up. I didn't see Katherine for the rest of that day. She was holed up in her room. We had dinner and then did much the same things that we usually do. Dancers don't stay in a pack. We all have our own interests. I hung around downstairs for a bit and then came up here about ten. Did some exercises, had a shower, tumbled into bed. I had a pile of novels I'd been looking over. I'm not much of a reader but I thought I'd better get some ideas about construction to help David with his when I persuade him to write it. Afraid they didn't hold my interest and I went sound asleep and stayed that way until morning."

"Your father?"

"After dinner he closed himself up in his study. I looked in on him before I came up and he wanted to tell me all about the paper he was writing—some project about the Masai. He said he worked until after eleven and then went to his quarters and to bed. Carl was up in his suite brooding over his buttons and the Lark told the police she was in her sitting room on the main floor. She said she watched—"

"Yes." Forsythe got to his feet. "We can get these details

54

from Mrs. Larkin and her brother. Would it have been difficult for any of you to leave the house unobserved?"

"Nothing easier. Katherine came down, took the key for Mandalay from the table in the hall, and left with nobody the wiser. Dozens of ways to get in and out of here. Long windows you can step out of on the main floor. Two staircases. This is a big place, Mr. Forsythe, and so few people in it."

"Have you a theory on the murder?"

She pulled herself up and faced him. "When they picked up that Fred Small I thought it must have been he. But he had an unbreakable alibi. Then I remembered the old woman that Katherine had killed. I thought of her son. But the police checked him out and he was in Germany. Now, I don't know what to think. The key was returned to its exact location . . . I simply don't know." The close-set eyes blazed up at Forsythe. "Whoever killed Katherine should get a medal! That woman was a menace. The world is the better without her."

"I can't argue about her character or her worth." Forsythe's face was cold and so was his voice. "But Katherine St. Croix was brutally murdered and that murderer is at large. The first killing is always the easiest."

"You think that one of us did it, don't you?" Cassandra drew herself to her full height. "Dancers have *killed*. Relatives of mine were in Africa and India. In many wars they died defending their country. But Dancers don't *murder*." She turned her back. "Show yourselves out!"

CHAPTER FIVE

MISS SANDERSON SPRAWLED ON THE LEATHER SOFA contentedly sipping a large whiskey and soda. Forsythe had settled on a matching chair and was working on his own drink. The curtains hadn't been pulled across the narrow windows and darkness crowded up against their panes like an unwelcome visitor. "How do you like your room, Sandy? Still Tom Jones?"

"Decidedly so. I had a few qualms when I saw the bed. Huge thing you can picture Henry the Eighth bedding down in. Luckily the mattress is new. Rather wish Mr. Bantam hadn't stuck to tradition with the bathroom, tub large enough for three and a pathetic trickle of hot water. But I can't quarrel with this room. Snuggery is a good name for it. All we need is rain lashing against the window and a crackling fire on the hearth."

"Sounds more like Christmastime than July. Hungry?"

"Famished. Do you realize Cassandra Dancer didn't even offer tea?"

"From the description of Mrs. Larkin's cooking that may have been a mercy. Mr. Bantam tells me supper will be served in good time. No choice, of course."

Miss Sanderson rubbed her stomach. "Right now I could eat that boiled shoe leather Cassandra was mentioning." She sat up and slid her feet to the floor. "Ah, food!"

A chubby maid bearing a laden tray pushed open the door. Behind her Mr. Bantam balanced a smaller tray on his swelling paunch. The maid wore a wide smile and a velvet bow bobbed in frizzy fair hair directly above one eye. It looked like a blue butterfly poised for flight. Setting down the tray on a side table she laid the cloth and proceeded to arrange the dishes. Her employer contributed a coffee pot, two balloon glasses, and a squat bottle. Mr. Bantam told them jovially, "Thought you might care for a nip of brandy with your coffee, folks. How did you find the Dancers?"

"Appeared to be fine," Forsythe said.

"Townspeople are glad you're here, Mr. Forsythe. All of us are hoping you'll clear this dirty business up. Makes us look bad, you know."

Miss Sanderson's eyes widened. "How do you know why we're here?"

He chuckled, the sound rippling up from his paunch, reminding Forsythe of Willis Seton. "News travels fast in a place this size, miss. George Clark out to the Priory told our Nell all about you being invited to come out to the place. Didn't he, girl?"

Nell blushed to the roots of her frizzy hair. "George said you folks were going to find the maniac who did that girl in, sir."

"The reporters have given you a bad time?" Forsythe asked.

"Reporters and police and curiosity seekers." Mr. Bantam rubbed a hand over his gleaming skull. "Full of questions. Didn't get much from us. May not care overly for Dancers but we don't gossip to outsiders. Don't wash dirty linen in public." He nudged the maid toward the door and followed her. "Need anything else, ring. Nell will look after you. Bar keeps me hopping. Folks flooding in."

57

He closed the door softly and Miss Sanderson shook her head. "It's a good thing we're not working undercover, Robby. About as much privacy as a fish tank." Losing interest in the innkeeper, she inspected the contents of the covered dishes. "Roast beef and Yorkshire pudding. Dig in."

They applied themselves to generous helpings and conversation languished. Scraping up the last morsel of apple crisp, Miss Sanderson reached for the cheese board. "The missus is better than a fair to middling cook, Robby. I can see where our host gets his girth." She accepted coffee and brandy and leaned back. "I suppose tomorrow we go back to the Priory and interview the rest of the household."

Forsythe was packing his pipe bowl. "We'll have a change of pace, Sandy. Concentrate on Harper. Ring up Miss Prudence Pyne and David Proctor and don't let them put you off. If necessary be pressing."

Holding up the balloon glass, Miss Sanderson wistfully looked into its amber depths. "David Proctor is one man I really wouldn't mind pressing, Robby."

As they passed the stone lion reclining on the grass, Miss Sanderson patted its noble head. Catching her employer's eye, she jerked her head at a window. Peeking out between lace curtains a sign announced that bed and breakfast was available within. Before they reached the steps the door opened and a stout woman bounced out. "The Widow Hawkins," Miss Sanderson muttered. "Cupboard-size rooms and an outdoor w.c."

The widow wore a girlish ruffled dress, had girlish curls clustered on a round head, and had applied lavish amounts of pink lip rouge. Her voice matched her appearance, shrill and gushing and girlish. "David is waiting for you. Naughty boy, should be in his bed. Delicate chest, you see, and coming down with a cold. Nursed him through bad bouts all last winter. Come in, do come in."

They went into a tiny dark hall and the widow threw open a door to the left. "David," she cooed, "your company is here."

David didn't look ill. He sat in a spill of sunshine at a table in the curve of a bay window. The strong light was kind to his classic features and thick hair. He wore a shabby smoking jacket with a scarf at his throat. Before him was spread as lavish a breakfast as the one they had consumed at the Harper Arms. "Miss Sanderson," Proctor said and bent over Miss Sanderson's hand. "And Mr. Forsythe. Do make yourselves comfortable. Would you care . . ." He wafted a slender hand over the table.

"Thank you, no," Miss Sanderson simpered. Definitely simpered, Forsythe thought, and darted a look at her. Her thin face, usually so austere, was glowing.

"Rest," the widow said and pressed the young man firmly back in his chair. "I'll bring coffee for your guests. So delicate," she told Miss Sanderson as she passed her chair.

Miss Sanderson was regarding Proctor with concern. "If you're not feeling well this could have waited."

He touched his chest. "Always have bouts of bronchitis and rotten colds but Mrs. Hawkins makes rather too much of it. If I even cough she has me swaddled in flannel and mustard. Good woman though, and she's been marvelous to me."

Silently the barrister agreed. The room was large and well furnished. It smelled of furniture polish and all surfaces gleamed. Proctor followed Forsythe's eyes complacently. "That door leads to the bath and the one next to it to the bedroom. The police were most interested in the third. Leads directly to the garden. Mrs. Hawkins had this suite made up for her father and he was an independent old chap. Insisted on going and coming without tracking through the rest of the house. Police made a big thing about me being able to slip in and out unobserved."

Mrs. Hawkins, bustling back with a coffee pot and extra cups, caught the last few words. "Terrible people," she said indignantly. "Told that inspector that David is a perfect lamb. Wouldn't sneak around bashing girls' heads in. Not my David."

Proctor gave his landlady a bewitching smile and her fat face pinkened with pleasure. "You defended me nobly. For a time I thought you might bean the inspector with your skillet." He added firmly, "That's lovely, Mrs. Hawkins."

She took the hint and left them. Proctor gave a rueful laugh. "So, I'll start by telling you I have no alibi for the night of Miss St. Croix's death. I was here working. Also, when I don't wish to be disturbed I put a pink card on the door. When that card is there Mrs. Hawkins leaves me strictly alone. That night the card was on the door. However, as I told the inspector, I worked until after midnight and then went to bed."

"You remember the night clearly," Forsythe said, "yet it was over two months ago."

The young man spread marmalade lavishly on a muffin. "You must realize the following day when I went to the Priory the family was in an uproar. During the night Katherine had taken off. Rather sets the circumstances in one's mind."

"Like John Kennedy's assassination," Miss Sanderson murmured.

"Exactly. On a much smaller scale, of course."

Forsythe again darted a look at his secretary's bemused expression. Proctor appeared to have a profound effect on women. "Were you surprised that Miss St. Croix had left so unexpectedly?"

"Astounded. I knew little about the woman but she seemed to be settling in nicely with the Dancers and there had been no hint of her leaving. After her body was discovered in Mandalay and Cassandra had to tell the police

60

about her investigation of the woman's past, the reason for her hasty departure was quite clear."

"Miss Dancer didn't let on to you what she'd discovered?"

"Didn't say a word. Cass can be closemouthed and we'd had a heated argument about Katherine a few days before. You'll want to know about my relations with the dead woman. I had a devil of a time recalling the dates when I saw her. Oh, we'd passed a number of times when I went out to play for Cass but Katherine did come in to Harper to see me twice." He poured coffee and handed the cups around. "The first time was on a Monday. The second on the following Thursday. Cass exploded when she found out about the Monday visit and that's when we quarreled. Quite frankly I thought it was *my* business and Katherine seemed to be a harmless person."

"She wanted advice on her book?"

"Katherine hadn't a clue on how to get the actual writing started. She said she was a great reader and fairly good at research, but she did need help getting her notes in order. She knew that I am a published writer—"

"Really," Miss Sanderson exclaimed, "how exciting."

"Far from exciting, dear lady. A few poems in little publications and this." He reached for a bookshelf and took down a slim volume bound in violet-colored leather. "Privately printed. Viola Dancer made the arrangements. Perhaps you'd care to borrow it and look it over."

Miss Sanderson tenderly deposited the book on her lap along with her copious handbag. Forsythe wondered if she'd had sense enough to turn on her tape or snooper as she called it. He tried to catch her eyes but she was staring at Proctor as though he were the Holy Grail. Women, Forsythe thought wrathfully. "Are you and Miss Dancer engaged?" Forsythe asked.

"Not formally. Cass would have been willing to marry a

few weeks after her mother's death but I couldn't see it. Wouldn't have looked well, you know."

"But you are in love?" Miss Sanderson gushed.

"Cass is. I've been quite frank with the girl. I don't love her. She has a fine nature but she's not terribly attractive. Viola not only had a beautiful nature but she was lovely. Considerably older than I but she had heavenly looks. Misty dark hair, great dark eyes, and a skin like . . . Tall and slim and elegant. I loved Viola and if she had lived . . ."

"Lady Dancer acted as your patron?" Forsythe asked.

"She did. We met at a poetry reading in London, not mine—I was in the audience. Viola sat down beside me and we got into a bit of a discussion about the poems. One thing led to another and afterward we went for a drink. Viola found I wrote a little poetry and asked me all about myself. Quite flattering for a young chap to have a beautiful older woman interested in him. Elegantly dressed too. Clothes that quietly shrieked money. I confessed I had a silly job selling insurance and lived in a dingy room. After that . . ." Proctor leaned back and crossed his legs. "She came up to see me in London several times and suggested I chuck my job and devote myself to writing full time. Viola insisted I come to her country home."

"To the Priory?"

"At the time I assumed she meant the Priory. It wasn't until I got down here that I found she'd made arrangements with Mrs. Hawkins for this place. I'll admit I was far from pleased." At the memory David Proctor looked far from pleased. His mouth, Forsythe noticed, was definitely petulant. "I also assumed Viola would be taking care of my expenses. But she paid my rent for only two months and then insisted I start giving music lessons to the country brats. She told me it would be much better for my self-esteem if I earned my own way." Sighing heavily, Proctor said, "As I have written,

O woman! in our hours of ease,
Uncertain, coy, and hard to please,
And variable as the shade
By the light quivering aspen made; . . ."

"That," Miss Sanderson said sharply, "is not David Proctor. It's Sir Walter Scott."

Proctor looked faintly surprised. "How discerning of you."

She gave him a wicked grin. "Try this. 'I'm not denyin' women are foolish: God Almighty made 'em to match the men.'"

"I'm afraid, Miss Sanderson, I can't quite place that quote."

"George Eliot," she said smugly and moved the leather covered book from her lap to the table at her elbow.

Ah, Forsythe thought, Sandy is getting her wits about her again. He turned his attention back to the poet. "Did Lady Dancer not assist you at all?"

"Once in a while she'd give me a small gift of money. And on my birthday and at Christmas she gave me expensive presents—a wonderful watch, Patek, a gold cigarette case and trifles like that. I had them stolen from me in a hotel in London. Cass and I had driven up and I stayed over to see a publisher about a couple of poems he showed interest in. Serves me right. That hotel was a sleazy hole. Mistake to stay there."

"Miss Dancer mentioned that," Forsythe told him. "That was the day she picked up the background information on Miss St. Croix."

"Cass is madly practical. Right now she insists I work on a novel. She may be right too. No money in poetry."

Miss Sanderson lifted her brows. "Money is important to you?"

"Major importance. I know all the myths about true artists preferring to starve but that's pure fiction. I've never

63

seen any reason why art can't be produced when one is in comfortable circumstances. My marriage to Cass will take care of that. She has her own money and we'll take a nice house and . . ."

Miss Sanderson was looking like a thundercloud so Forsythe said hastily, "Lady Dancer was contemplating divorce at the time of her death?"

"If she'd lived she would have divorced Sir Amyas. Viola admitted she despised him. I rather like the man and he's been decent to me but they should never have married. Viola was a mere child at the time and her father bartered her off like a horse for a title. Horace Gillimede has lived to regret that. Yes, Viola and I were in love and we would have had a meaningful life. She was so sensitive, so attuned to art. There's a little poem I wrote to her in that book, Miss Sanderson. You'll enjoy it. It's called 'Violet, My Violet.' I always thought of her as a violet—shy and sweet and hiding her beauty from the eyes of the world." He rubbed his brow, pushing back the lock of hair that fell there. When he removed his hand it promptly fell back into place. "When Carl carried his mother out of the lake my heart broke. She lay there at our feet, her hair plastered down like seaweed against her face. Horace was howling like a wolf. He was literally tearing at her sailor suit."

Bending forward, the young man buried his face in his hands. "She must have had that suit made for me. I've always been afraid of water. Had a bad experience when I was a child. Viola was just as afraid. We talked about it and decided we must overcome our weakness. Viola must have wanted to show me her courage and she knew nothing about boats . . . not the first thing."

Forsythe frowned. "Why was Horace Gillimede tearing at the sailor suit?"

"God knows. The old fellow is bonkers, you know." Proctor uncovered his face. "He was ranting on about it being the instrument of the devil. He kept it up and none of us knew what to do. Then the aunts arrived and Miss Sybil calmed the poor devil down. She sent Mrs. Larkin to get a dressing gown and blankets and then Miss Sybil and Miss Bella stripped off the sailor outfit and gave it to Horace. He even took the little white cap. Then he went bolting into the woods crying that he must destroy the devil's work. It was simply horrible."

"Could Lady Dancer have committed suicide?" the barrister asked.

"No! Viola adored life! It was an accident."

"You think she was planning to divorce her husband?"

"I *know* she was. On her birthday morning she phoned me. I naturally thought I would be invited for dinner but Viola said I wasn't to come. She said she wanted to dine with her family that evening. Viola assured me the next day she would have news for me. I knew she'd finally come around and decided to chuck Sir Amyas."

"Did she say so?"

"Not in so many words. But she hinted about it and she sounded so happy and relieved."

"How would her family have accepted the divorce?"

"Sir Amyas would have been as happy as I was. He cared no more for Viola than she for him. The rest of them were dead set against it."

Miss Sanderson leaned forward. "But divorce is so common."

"Not for Dancers. For them it's a deadly sin. No Dancer has ever divorced."

"Surely Cassandra doesn't feel that way."

He smiled at Miss Sanderson. "Cass was only worried about her mother being free to marry me. She tells me she had her sights set on me from the moment we met. Kept warning me Viola would destroy my writing ability."

Making a sound suspiciously like a snort, Miss Sanderson settled back.

The barrister said, "Can you think of anything, Mr.

Proctor, any small thing about Miss St. Croix that might help us?"

Bracing an elbow on the table, Proctor lowered his chin onto the back of his hand and appeared to be deep in thought. It was a graceful posture and showed off the lines of his head and face to good advantage. After a time he said slowly, "I believe I've told you all I know about her. Little things . . . she was easy on the eyes and had a reserved, ladylike manner. At the time I would have described her as prim, even prudish. Now that I know Katherine's past I can only say she was crafty and one hell of a good actress." He raised his head. "Sorry, that's all I can tell you."

"Have you any idea who could have killed her?"

"I'm torn two ways. On one hand I'd like to think it was that criminal element she was mixed up with. But the evidence doesn't point that way. I'm completely baffled."

Forsythe got to his feet and as he did he noticed that Miss Sanderson's hand was fumbling in her handbag. She had remembered to turn on her snooper. "Thank you, Mr. Proctor. If you should think of anything else we can be reached at the Harper Arms."

Proctor offered the barrister a hand and his secretary a bewitching smile. Forsythe accepted the hand but Miss Sanderson ignored the smile. This time as they passed the sprawling lion she didn't pat it. They walked along slowly. As they neared the corner and the ancient church Forsythe noticed that Miss Sanderson didn't even glance in its direction. Her head was bent and she appeared to be eyeing her sensible brogues as they marched over the cobblestones. "You forgot the book of poems," he pointed out.

"So I did," she said indifferently.

"Do I detect an aura of disillusionment?"

"Disgust. A young Lord Byron!" She snorted, this time loudly.

"Because the man tried to pretend Scott's work was his own?"

66

"Because the man is nothing but a pretty face balanced on a monstrous ego. Robby, when he lost Viola and her marriage settlement he immediately fastened onto Cassandra and her grandfather's legacy."

"I'm inclined to think Cassandra fastened onto *him*."

"The girl must be a fool."

"I doubt that. What time will we be seeing Miss Pyne?"

"She invited us for tea. We just passed her house." Miss Sanderson turned and pointed. "That white Victorian opposite the church. Nice house and she has a nice voice." She added gloomily, "With our luck her voice will be the only nice thing about her."

CHAPTER SIX

Not only the exterior of the house was nice but so was the parlor in which Forsythe and Miss Sanderson were comfortably seated. It was a good-sized room, filled with furniture of the Victorian era, and it was well cared for but not stiff. Over the fireplace hung a poster by Toulouse-Lautrec. It looked rather exotic among velvet swags, antimacassars and whatnots. Miss Prudence Pyne, dispensing tea and conversation from behind the tea table, was, as David Proctor would have said, pleasing to the eyes.

"Yes," she was saying, "I consider myself a newcomer to Harper. Most of the villagers' families have been here almost as long as the Dancer family. The Pyne ancestry in this village dates only back to my grandparents."

Forsythe regarded her with pleasure. Her fine skin was cobwebbed with wrinkles and the delicate hands hovering over the tea table were marred with rusty marks of age but there was something incredibly youthful about her. She wore a gray tweed skirt, a rose twin set, and sturdy shoes, but her legs were excellent and her bright blue eyes were unfaded by time. In her younger days Prudence Pyne must have been a beauty.

Miss Sanderson accepted her cup and selected a fairy cake from the tiered cake plate. "You have known the Dancer family for a long time?"

"All my life. I clearly remember Amyas' father Sir Crawford and his wife, Dora. Sir Crawford was much like his son but Dora, although regrettably plain, had a fine mind and was an excellent businesswoman. Dora was the one who urged her husband before his death to set aside funds for his daughters and his grandchildren. I believe Dora was fond of Amyas but she knew he was hopeless when it came to money management. Amyas allows money to trickle through his fingers. I do hope his oil money is as inexhaustible as he acts."

Miss Sanderson nodded. "You've heard about the amphitheater?"

"Oh, yes. I suppose one should be glad he hasn't set his heart on a replica of the Taj Mahal."

"Or the Leaning Tower of Pisa."

Miss Pyne's eyes sparkled with mischief. "To say nothing of the Hanging Gardens of Babylon."

Forsythe gazed from one woman to the other. They were regarding each other with delight. Kindred spirits, he thought. Miss Pyne leaned toward the younger woman and asked, "Have you heard about the famous fox hunt?"

"A few details. How I wish I could have seen it!"

"I did."

"Really?"

"A balcony seat for the hunt. Literally. I was chairing a meeting of the Women's Institute and we have rooms in that large building as you enter Harper, at the foot of the high street. The windows were open and suddenly there was this perfect din. Voices holloing and horns blowing. All the ladies crowded out on the balcony in time to see Amyas leading the group of thundering nudes. Oh, my dear!" Cupping a hand over her mouth, Miss Pyne quivered with mirth.

"Do tell us," Miss Sanderson implored.

"It was the high point of my life. I didn't dare let on, of course. The other ladies were scandalized; one fainted, and I had to pretend to be shocked. But when I looked down and saw the hounds bounding along and the riders shouting tallyho . . . you should have seen the buttocks and breasts bouncing. And there was Amyas with a wide smile and a derby tilted over one eye, having the time of his life. It was simply marvelous!"

Miss Sanderson had collapsed into helpless laughter and Forsythe asked with a smile, "And from that moment on the Dancers were not welcome in Harper?"

"There have always been strained relationships between the village and the Priory. Dancers have scandalized the locals for centuries. At the same time I believe the people here have a perverse kind of pride in the Dancers. You may deplore them but you must admit they can't be ignored."

"How do you regard them?"

"With a great deal of affection. I discovered their secret long ago. They're simply a group of people who reach adolescence and then stay there. Their actions and reactions are those of children. I find them rather endearing people. Admittedly they try one's patience but they're never boring. I'm speaking of true Dancers, of course. Once in a while one comes along who eventually grows up. Cassandra is very young but she has her grandmother Dora's common sense and I should imagine business sense. However, Cassandra's attachment to young Mr. Proctor certainly doesn't prove my point. I'm so hoping she will change her mind about that man."

Miss Sanderson regarded her hostess approvingly. "I take it you don't like David?"

"How can one? He has quite enough liking for himself. Completely self-centered and I've always thought he would have made an excellent mate for Viola Dancer. She was his female counterpart."

70

"Cassandra told us her mother often came to talk with you, Miss Pyne."

"Indeed she did. All Dancers come to me—even Carleton. But Viola didn't talk *with* one, she talked *at* one. Completely absorbed and delighted with her own feelings, her own problems. Amyas and she should never have married. In fact it would have been better if Amyas had remained a bachelor. There's simply no place in his life for either wives or children. I'm being very candid, Mr. Forsythe, but I should imagine that is what you wish."

Forsythe nodded. "It's the only thing that can help us. We know nothing about the Dancers and to get to the bottom of this tragedy we must look to the past. We must understand the people who were involved with Miss St. Croix."

Touching the short silver hair that clung to the lines of her finely shaped head, she said softly, "I understand that. The past never really dies, does it? Now, how to make you understand Viola? She was very lovely and dressed to complement her romantic beauty. But underneath she was quite different. Viola had a great thirst for power. For a time she tried to dominate her family. With Carleton she succeeded. Viola was the only mother the boy ever remembered and their relationship was far from healthy. Viola was the embodiment of Carleton's ideal woman. The boy worshiped her. But when she contemplated divorce, in his eyes, Viola fell from her pedestal."

"This seems incredible," Miss Sanderson said. "Carleton had a rock band and yet you speak of him as though he has the values of the eighteenth century."

"Strip the modern veneer from him, my dear, and you will find a man from an earlier, more romantic age. Carleton was outraged that this perfect woman could even consider leaving his father and entering into an association with a man of his own age." Miss Pyne sighed. "Viola appeared to require victims."

"Her protégés?" Forsythe asked.

"Exactly. Viola's first power play was with a young curate who was at St. Jude. His name was Hopkins and he was a nervous, moody man. Hopkins painted as a hobby, and poorly I fear, but Viola took him up and persuaded him he was on a par with Rembrandt or Van Gogh. Then, without warning, she dropped him cold. Hopkins gave up his post and went to Liverpool. I heard he fell into drink and bad company and eventually committed suicide. After that Viola had a succession of protégés. She treated them the same way. Lavished attention on them, let them fall in love with her, and then discarded them and went on to another."

"She did treat David Proctor rather shabbily," Miss Sanderson admitted.

"Yes. Viola enticed the young man down here on false pretenses. Mr. Proctor thought his future was assured and he soon found he was only a toy. Viola was rapidly losing interest in him when she discovered Cassandra was much attracted to Mr. Proctor; that revitalized her mother's interest."

"Dog in the manger?" Forsythe asked.

"Similar."

"Do you think Proctor really did love Lady Dancer?"

Miss Pyne touched her chin with a slender finger. "As much as his nature allows, I suppose he did. She was lovely, as I said, and doubtless physically appealing to the opposite sex. Cassandra, poor child, is a plain as Dora was. As soon as Viola sensed her daughter's interest in Mr. Proctor she took him up again. She talked to me at great length on her love for him, how torn she was between her duty and that love."

"Had she made up her mind to marry Proctor?"

"I'm inclined to think so. Viola was here the day before her birthday and she seemed much different. In fact she said she was through soul-searching, she was going to live her life as she wished. Yes, Mr. Forsythe, I'm positive she was going to divorce Amyas." The bright eyes caught the barrister's. "Would you like my opinion of the other members of the family?"

"Please."

"I've touched on both children. Cassandra hungers to marry Mr. Proctor and manage his career. Carleton contents himself with his button collection. In time that will pass. No doubt he will decide to row across the Atlantic or something of the sort. The Dancer sisters will continue their lives—"

"I understand they are quiet women," Miss Sanderson said.

"They live quiet lives but they are Dancers. Sybil is the elder and she completely dominates Bella. Sybil is highly intelligent and Bella on the dull side. Bella's whole mental processes revolve around cooking, cleaning, and gardening. Sybil's . . . well, you'll soon discover hers." Miss Pyne darted an impish smile at Miss Sanderson. "They were both pretty girls but Sybil had an unfortunate love affair and never married. So, of course, neither did Bella. Too bad. Bella would have made a wonderful wife for a man not interested in sparkling conversation. Sybil has a horror of modern devices. She refuses to keep a car and only had a telephone installed at the Dower House under protest."

"They do come in to see you," Forsythe said.

"Bella comes frequently. She's tremendously athletic and walks in to do the shopping. Generally she stops for a chat and to deliver some of her baked goods. She's really an inspired cook. Sybil comes once a month, on a Sunday for tea."

"Does Sybil walk in too?" Miss Sanderson asked.

"Heavens, no! An old chap who used to garden at the Priory hitches up an equally old mare to a cart and brings Sybil in style. I must admit I don't really look forward to these visits. Sybil can be a trial but it has been much more pleasant since she got rid of that dog she was convinced was her mother—"

73

"Now I believe you're joking," Miss Sanderson told the older woman.

Throwing back her head, Miss Pyne laughed. "I've let the cat out of the bag. I should have allowed you to meet Sybil and discover this for yourself, but Sybil is obsessed with a bewildering belief in reincarnation. She picked up this pup, a small nasty mongrel with bulging eyes, and became convinced her mother's spirit inhabited its rather smelly body. Every time Sybil came to visit me, the dog came too. She sat it on the chair, Miss Sanderson, that you're sitting on now and fed it cakes and tarts and so on. Madness can be contagious. After a time I found myself addressing the little beast as Dora."

"Sybil really *is* a Dancer," Miss Sanderson muttered.

"There's only one other person at the Priory, Horace Gillimede. Not a Dancer by birth but he fits in marvelously well with the family. A pathetic old fellow, driven mad by guilt because of his wife's fall from grace and the manner of her death." Miss Pyne eyed Forsythe, his long narrow head, and his slender body in impeccable tweeds. "I think *you* will see past Horace's wild appearance and wild words, Mr. Forsythe. Most people tend to write him off as a religious fanatic but some part of his mind operates on a sane level still." She folded her hands in her lap. "I could talk for hours about the Dancer family but—"

"That's fine, Miss Pyne," Forsythe assured her. "Could you tell us what you know about Miss St. Croix?"

"She had many names, I understand. I still think of her as Katie Parr. Do you mind if I use that name?"

"Of course not."

"This part of your interview I've been dreading. I hate to even think about the woman and to talk about her . . ." For a moment the rose-clad shoulders sagged, but then the old woman straightened them. "There is no excuse for me having admitted that woman to my house. I've handled servants all my life and, as my mother taught me, have been most cautious about references. I'd better find a place to begin. During my parents' lifetime we had a large staff. Through the years it dwindled down to Susan, the parlor maid, and the cook, Mary. To properly look after the place this was an inadequate number of servants but with taxes and inflation my income became pitifully small.

"We made out fairly well though and lived quite happily. Then, a year ago June, Mary died suddenly in her sleep. Neither Susan nor I had ever done much cooking. Oh, we can make a salad and scramble eggs but that is about all. And a capable cook in a small place like Harper is hard to find."

Forsythe said, "I understand from the police reports that Susan was the one who brought Miss St. Croix to the house."

"She was. On her free day Susan goes to Chester for her weekly treat. She takes the four o'clock bus into the city, has supper at a cafe, goes to the cinema for the evening, and returns to Harper on the bus at eleven. Susan is a friend of the proprietor of the cafe and knows the waitresses well. They chat to her about her job and me and so on. Susan is a great talker. After Mary's death they asked her frequently whether we'd found another cook and no doubt teased Susan about her lack of culinary skills."

"And that cafe is where Miss St. Croix heard about you and this house?"

"It must have been. Susan can't remember seeing the woman there but Katie must have been sitting in a corner— it's a busy place—and overheard. Anyway, about the middle of July Susan went in for her treat as usual and that night she did notice a pretty girl in a corner, having coffee and reading a book. Susan chattered on about her mistress not getting a decent meal without a cook and so on. After the film Susan caught the bus back and the same girl got on it. She sat down in front of Susan and when the bus stopped in front of the Harper Arms Susan was surprised to see the girl get off.

Except for locals, few travelers stop at that time of night in the village.

"The girl stood looking around as though she were lost, and Susan, who's a kindhearted soul, asked whether she needed directions. Katie Parr inquired whether there was a youth hostel in the village and Susan said no, there was only the Harper Arms and the Widow Hawkins', but she probably could get a room in one of them. The girl told her the only reason she'd gotten off the bus was that she had no money to continue and couldn't pay for a room. Susan was distressed at the girl's plight and even more so when Katie started swaying around and clutched at her arm for support."

"Because she hadn't eaten in several days," Miss Sanderson said caustically.

"Exactly. Susan felt she couldn't leave the girl there and so she brought her home to me. I always wait up for Susan and when they arrived the girl did look sick so I sent Susan to warm up some tinned soup." Miss Pyne's lips set in a bitter line. "That was where I made my first mistake. I should have given her a little money and sent her on her way. But Katie Parr played the part of a timid, sweet orphan magnificently. I couldn't turn her out. Susan took her up to a room and I thought after breakfast the next day I'd send her on her way."

"It didn't work out that way?" Forsythe said.

"My second mistake was in letting my gluttony get in the way of common sense. I have never been a large eater, but I do relish well-cooked, attractively served food. For over a month I'd been existing on tinned food and scrambled eggs. The next morning when I arose I smelt the most heavenly odors. Katie had got up early and to earn her night's keep had cooked breakfast. You should have seen that breakfast! Waffles and bacon and sausage. Grilled tomatoes and an omelet made with apricot preserve."

"A clever woman," Miss Sanderson muttered.

"And a marvelous cook. I questioned Katie about her past. She told me she'd been a cook for a family in Birmingham until they had left the country. She said she was on her way to London to get another job but her savings were exhausted. So, without asking about references, I literally begged her to stay with us for a time. I assured her she could save her wages and then go her way. She agreed. As Horace Gillimede would say, I had opened my door to a devil.

"For a week all went well. Susan and Katie got along well and I was so happy with the meals. If I hadn't been such an idiot I would have noticed something rather odd. Katie never set foot out of this house. Part of her duties was the food shopping and she didn't refuse to do it, she merely made excuses so Susan would have to."

Forsythe jerked his head up. "Sounds as though she didn't want anyone to be able to recognize her."

"Quite. Katie must have already been planning to move in on the Dancers. She knew by that time that I seldom go to the Priory so she wasn't worried about Susan or me. But she didn't want the villagers to remember her. Strange . . ."

"What are you thinking?"

"Time. Katie left us in early August. In fact it was August the third. The reason I remember the date is because Viola had died two days before and then that dreadful scene with Katie Parr. Rather sticks in the mind. But, Mr. Forsythe, it wasn't until last April that Katie managed to get into the Priory. Why the delay?"

"A puzzling question, Miss Pyne. Why did the woman wait eight months before approaching the Dancer family? Was it because of Lady Dancer's death? Did Miss St. Croix not wish to disturb the family while they were in mourning?"

Miss Pyne said dryly, "I hardly credit Katie Parr with that kind of sensitivity."

"Would it be possible to ask your maid a few questions?"

The old woman hesitated and then said, "I'd really rather you didn't. Susan is such a nervous woman and she's relived the whole business since the woman's body was discovered."

"Miss Sanderson and I don't practice third degree, Miss Pyne."

"Of course you don't. How silly of me." Reaching for a silver hand bell, she tinkled it.

In moments the door of the parlor creaked open and a trimly uniformed maid took a step into the room. Susan looked sixtyish and her most outstanding features were kindly eyes behind thick glasses and a sharp pink-tipped nose. Her mouth was quivering as she said, "You want me, Miss Pru?"

"This is Miss Sanderson and Mr. Forsythe, Susan. Mr. Forsythe would like to ask you some questions about Katie."

The maid's mouth continued quivering and the pink nostrils flared like a frightened mare's. "It's all my fault!" she wailed. "I wished that awful creature on Miss Pru and the Dancer family!"

"Come now, Susan." With a light, youthful movement Prudence Pyne rose and drew the maid to a chair facing the barrister. "We've discussed that many times and it's certainly not your fault. Do sit down, silly girl, and relax."

Susan perched on the edge of the chair and regarded Forsythe with the fascination a cornered rabbit might show for a vicious dog. Forsythe gave her a reassuring smile and said gently, "I should imagine you miss Mary, Susan."

"I do. Like sisters we were." The kind eyes behind the heavy lenses misted and her mistress pressed a lace-trimmed hankie into her hand. "When our work was done Mary and me would sit in the kitchen and talk. We watched my telly every night and . . ."

"You must have been lonely after Mary's death. Did you find Katie Parr good company?"

The maid flinched when he said the name and Miss Pyne put a comforting hand on her shoulder. "She . . . she liked to hear me talk. Guess maybe I was kind of proud such a pretty girl would hang on every word I said. She didn't talk much but I did."

"What did you talk about?"

"She wanted to hear about people in the village. Where they lived and what they did. First off she said she thought when she saw this house that the mistress must have lots of money. And I told her no, Miss Pru doesn't have much. Then we got chatting about people who still have bags of money."

"And that's when the Dancers' name came up?"

"Kind of. She never went out but we were looking out the window and I saw young Mr. Proctor who stays with the widow down the road a piece and I says, 'that's a poet and isn't he good looking.' Katie she says, 'he sure is and does he have money?' And I says, 'no, but Lady Dancer looks after him.' And Katie says . . . that's when I told her all about the Dancers."

"Did Katie Parr see any of the Dancer family?"

"They was always in and out. Katie never set foot out of the kitchen when folks came in but she was always peeking through the door when they was in the dining room. She seen Lady Dancer and Miss Cassandra and—" Susan peered up at her mistress. "Mr. Carleton was here too, wasn't he, Miss Pru?"

"He was. He dined with me the night that Cassandra was here. I believe Amyas was also in for tea one afternoon."

"That's right. Clean forgot about Sir Amyas. Kind of puffing myself up in front of Katie 'bout how much I knew about them."

Forsythe nodded. "You told Katie Parr about Carleton's button collection?"

"Right off. 'Bout that and his rock group. Told her about

Mr. Carleton going regular to Chester for that auction. Told her everything I knew!"

The rabbit nose and mouth were quivering convulsively and the maid was twisting her apron in both hands. Miss Pyne sent the barrister an imploring look and he said mildly, "That's fine, Susan. You've answered my questions marvelously. Thank you."

The maid lurched to her feet. "All my fault, sir! Brought this down on Miss Pru and the Dancer family."

Taking her arm, Forsythe piloted her to the door. "It isn't your fault, Susan. Katie Parr was a bad person. If you hadn't told her she would have found out elsewhere. Put this whole business out of your mind."

He returned to his chair and waited until Miss Pyne had seated herself behind the tea table. She smiled at him. "I'm grateful, Mr. Forsythe. You were very good with Susan. Now you understand how the woman knew so much about the Dancers."

"Yes. The reason she provided herself with those bone buttons shaped like skulls, her knowledge about the members of the family. It's quite clear. She used your house as a listening post to see whether there were people in Harper worth her peculiar talents." His long fingers tapped the arm of his chair. "You said for a week everything went smoothly. What happened then?"

"On the Monday I heard that Viola had drowned in the China Sea. Tuesday is only a blur in my memory. Elderly people feel so helpless, when faced with a close friend's death—almost guilty, as though it should be they who died and not a younger, more vital person. I didn't intrude on the family's grief but I did write a letter of condolence and I sent flowers. All the silly useless things one does at a time like that. Katie's meals that day were as good as ever but I could hardly swallow. Wednesday I remember clearly. I wish I could forget!"

Leaning her head back, Miss Pyne closed her eyes. The

color had drained from her face, leaving the wrinkled skin chalky. This is what she will look like when she is dead, Forsythe thought sadly. Without the vividly expressive eyes her face was skull-like, beautiful bones tautly covered with parchment. The bone structure was remarkably lovely and strong. He didn't prompt her and finally she said, "I will tell you everything. I didn't . . . I couldn't force myself to tell Inspector Fitzgerald some of this but . . ." Her eyelids lifted and she looked directly into the barrister's eyes. "In the morning I went out to work in the garden. I can't afford a gardener and the neglect bothers me. I was puttering around, doing some weeding, when my neighbor leaned across the fence.

"Mrs. Froud is a nice young person with three tiny children, and very busy with the wee ones. She is not a gossip and I've grown fond of her. I could see she was perturbed and uncertain but finally she said that the week before her youngest child had been ill, a stomach upset, and she'd been up and down all night with the tot. She'd glanced out the nursery window, which faces on the side of this house, and had seen Katie Parr climb out of her window, down to an attached shed, and then drop to the ground like a cat. Mrs. Froud wasn't sure of the time but my house was dark and she knew Susan and I were in bed. She also said this hadn't been the first time Katie had left that way. Mr. Froud had been working late another night and had also seen her. Mr. Froud had advised his wife to tell me about it but she had hesitated, thinking I might consider her a meddler."

Forsythe's brow wrinkled in thought. "Had you forbidden Katie to leave the house in the evenings?"

"Of course not! I'm not a jailer, Mr. Forsythe. I had told the girl to come and go as she liked, but I did ask her to let me know when she left the house after nine. One has to know where the servants are."

"What did you think?"

"I found Katie's conduct quite inexplicable. I thought perhaps she might be sneaking out to see a boy but—" Miss Pyne smiled wryly. "I returned to the house to ask an explanation but I'm afraid I did procrastinate. The meals, you know, I hated to lose her. So instead of going to her I went to my desk, over there." Miss Pyne pointed at a highly polished rosewood desk. "On Wednesdays I always bring my household accounts up-to-date. I am meticulous, as my mother trained me; I keep account of everything spent. When the accounts were tallied I balanced the figure against the money in the cash box. This is a small wooden box used long ago for stationery. No, I can see the question trembling on your lips. It had no lock. There had never been any reason to lock up the household money. Both Mary and Susan were absolutely honest. But that day twenty pounds was missing. I checked my figures and I knew there was no possibility of a mistake."

"And that is when you questioned Katie Parr?"

"I rang for her and she came in here. Looking at the girl, so meek and mild and respectful, I simply couldn't believe she was a sneak and a thief. But I told her what Mrs. Froud had said and asked for an explanation. Her mask, I suppose you would call it that, fell away and I truly saw the woman for the first time. She was simply dreadful.

"Katie flew into a rage and I'll admit I was afraid she might attack me. She told me Susan and I were old and should be dead and that it was no fun to live in a house with a couple of corpses. She said it was her business how she left the house. Her language . . . I've read the words, Mr. Forsythe, and hearing them didn't shock me as much as the way she said them. As though she *thought* in that dreadful way."

Miss Pyne paused and Miss Sanderson gave an involuntary sound of sympathy. "It must have been *awful* for you."

"It was, Miss Sanderson." Miss Pyne's chin lifted. "But I am not without courage and so I told her she was also a thief and I would have to call on the police to deal with her. I told her there was money missing from my desk. Then her anger appeared to vanish. Katie said if I called in the police she would tell them she saw *Susan* taking the money. I told her Susan had been with me for almost forty years and in that time she hadn't taken a shilling. Then . . ."

"Yes?" Forsythe gently prompted.

"This is what I didn't tell Inspector Fitzgerald. Katie smiled and I still remember that smile. She leaned across the desk and I could feel her breath touching my face. She whispered. She said she would tell the police that Susan and I . . . that there was an unnatural relationship between us. That I went to Susan's room and—"

"I understand." Forsythe leaned across the table and patted a fragile, age-spotted hand.

"I felt as though this room, this house, had been covered with slime. As though Katie Parr had encased me with *filth*. I couldn't fight her. As soon as I could speak I told her to leave, to get out. To go and never let me see her face again. She went and with her she took the only pieces of my mother's jewelry I had left. A cameo brooch ringed with pearls and a garnet ring. Not valuable in terms of money but of inestimable value to me." Miss Pyne's head dropped like a silvery flower on a slender stem. "I didn't dare call the police to recover them!"

Leaning over, Miss Sanderson dug a sharp finger into the barrister's ribs but he didn't take the hint. "You've been candid with us, Miss Pyne, and I hate to bother you further but I must ask you a question. Who—"

"I know what your question is." The silvery head lifted, "The identity of the woman's murderer. Many of the villagers think it was someone from the woman's past and I would like to think that myself. But it's impossible. Whoever killed Katie Parr was no stranger to this area. The murderer was someone who knew the village and the Dancer estate, knew the Priory and the grounds, knew about

Mandalay, knew the key to the temple was kept in the table in the entrance hall. That narrows it down to a member of the Dancer family or someone who visited the house frequently. The Dancers don't have many locals in the house. There are delivery people, of course, but they go to the tradesmen's door and don't enter the house. Doctor Beam and the vicar are there once in a while. Doctor Beam plays chess with Amyas and the vicar loves to argue with Horace Gillimede. Says it keeps him on his toes. But the night that Katie Parr was killed Doctor Beam was in Scotland visiting relatives. As for the vicar I can hardly picture a man of nearly ninety being that active and, of course, his nature goes against it."

"You've narrowed the suspects down, Miss Pyne."

"Yes. At the Priory are Amyas, the two children, Horace Gilimede, Sybil and Bella, and the servants. In Harper there are Mr. Proctor and myself. You will want to know my movements that Sunday evening. I attended the service at St. Jude, returned here at nine, and spent the rest of the evening reading. I have trouble sleeping and frequently go for long walks, hoping my sleep will be sounder. Susan, as soon as dinner was over and the kitchen straightened, went directly to her room to watch her television as she does every night."

"Did you walk that evening, Miss Pyne?"

"That night, Mr. Forsythe, I slept soundly. A better sleep than I'd had in months."

Miss Sanderson was prodding him again and this time Forsythe got to his feet. Miss Pyne rose with her light grace. "Two more questions and then we'll leave, Miss Pyne. When did you discover that Katie Parr and Katherine St. Croix were the same woman?"

"After the discovery of her body in the crypt a police constable came to my door. He had a picture of Katherine St. Croix. I told him she had worked for me as a cook for not quite a fortnight last year. Then Inspector Fitzgerald, who seemed a pleasant man, came and I told him most of what I've told you."

"And you had never connected Katie Parr and the woman Amyas had employed to write the family book?"

"I had only heard about Katherine St. Croix. Carleton and Cassandra and Amyas had mentioned a girl who had worked at a library and was at the Priory. All any of them said was that she was quite nice looking and seemed intelligent. There was certainly no reason to suspect it was my former cook."

Forsythe looked down at the elderly woman searchingly. "Why did you tell us the detail you had concealed from the police?"

"That's the third question, Mr. Forsythe. But I will answer it." She circled the table and stood at his side. One hand touched his sleeve. "I would urge you and Miss Sanderson to leave Harper and go back to your own lives. Let it go, Mr. Forsythe, let it go."

"The woman was murdered, Miss Pyne. Brutally murdered."

"Executed. There is a difference. Think of her past, Mr. Forsythe. Think of her victims. Think of the people like myself who welcomed her into their homes. Consider the way Katie Parr used decency and kindness against them. She used good instincts as weapons. I am *glad* she's dead. I am *happy* Katie Parr will never find another victim. She came into my house and she violated it. Katie Parr *violated* me."

Once outside Miss Pyne's house Miss Sanderson set off at a rapid pace. Even with the advantage of longer legs Forsythe had difficulty overtaking her. He managed to catch up with her as she passed the stone lion in front of the Widow Hawkins'. "Sandy," he panted, "you're going the wrong way."

Her low-heeled shoes hit the dirt road and tiny spurts of dust puffed up. "No, I'm not." She stopped abruptly and pointed. "Robby, there are the gates of the Priory. Not far from Miss Pyne's house."

"Not far."

"She said she walked at night. She said she didn't sleep well. When you asked Miss Pyne if she'd walked the night of Katherine St. Croix's murder she was evasive."

"She was indeed. She merely said she slept soundly."

His secretary's slender shoulders sagged. "Robby, could she have walked that night? Could she have walked to the Priory grounds? Could she have seen Katherine heading toward Mandalay and followed her? Could she have seen that woman *violating* the crypt?"

"To all your questions there is only one answer. Yes, she could have." He put an arm around the sagging shoulders and Miss Sanderson turned and buried her face against his shoulder. "Sandy, tell me what you're thinking."

"Let's drop this." Her voice was muffled. "Let's go back to London."

"I'll put you on a bus this evening. You go back."

"Not you?"

"I *have* to stay."

"Then we both do." Pulling away, Miss Sanderson kicked a rock and sent it careening into a hedge. "I like her, Robby. Miss Pyne is the kind of woman you'd like to have as a mother. She reminds me of an aunt I loved dearly. At times like this I *hate* what we do. Poking and prying!"

"I know." Forsythe's expression was somber. "Perhaps, Sandy, this is our destiny. If it is, we're quite powerless."

"Oh, hell!" Miss Sanderson wheeled and strode toward the high street.

CHAPTER SEVEN

"SINCE I HAVE BEEN VERY YOUNG I HAVE BELIEVED IN the force of destiny," Miss Sybil Dancer said firmly. 'No matter how an individual strives, one is condemned to complete a certain pattern. We have no control over our fate."

"All roads lead to Samaria," Robert Forsythe murmured.

"*Precisely.* I seldom take to strangers but the moment I glimpsed you on my doorstep I said, yes, Sybil, here is a Seeing Soul. I had a fantastic flash of precognition. You and I, Mr. Forsythe, in another life achieved a oneness. Do you feel this way, too?"

While Forsythe groped for words his secretary eyed the woman who was claiming a oneness with him. An unlikely pair, Miss Sanderson thought. Amyas Dancer's older sister was tall and possibly possessed a wiry build. Her figure could only be guessed at. From neck to heels the woman was swathed in a black satin garment resembling a tent. Her small head was covered by a black and yellow striped turban and one clawlike hand made great play with a silk fan. Against its black background the signs of the Zodiac were brilliantly detailed in yellow. She had a long scrawny neck and black beady eyes. Any beauty she had possessed as a girl had long since fled.

Instead of answering Sybil's question Forsythe countered with one of his own. "You feel we are not accountable for our own actions, Miss Sybil?"

"Of course we aren't! We merely play out our roles and then go on to another in yet another life. Wearying, but that is destiny. Ah, here is my sister. Bella, we're scarcely up from the lunch table and you are pressing food upon us."

Bella pushed the tea wagon into the prim little parlor of the Dower House and proceeded to unload it. Compared with her exotic sister, Bella looked prosaic. She had a build much like her brother—short and wide and muscular. She wore faded jeans, a cotton shirt, and Adidas sneakers. Graying hair fell in a single plait down her broad back. Both sisters had the handsome high-bridged Dancer nose. "I thought our visitors would welcome a snack after the walk from Harper, Sis."

Sybil waved the fan. "Only an excuse for you to stuff yourself. I'd swear if you didn't work as hard as you do you would be so heavy you would have to be trundled in a wheelbarrow." Turning back to Forsythe, she declared, "I eat like a bird, Mr. Forsythe. Do we share appetites, too?"

Forsythe was helping himself to hot cheese puffs and merely shook his head. His secretary, who had lunched on toast and coffee, helped herself liberally. Bella beamed at her and pushed a plate of butter tarts closer.

"Our mother was a smelly bitch," Sybil said flatly.

Miss Sanderson nearly dropped her cup and Forsythe gulped. "Sis means," Bella explained, "she thinks mother's spirit came back in a dog."

"It did. You remarked on the resemblance yourself."

"I did not! It was a bad-tempered thing and snapped at me and made messes on the carpet. Mother never bit me or made messes—"

"Don't be obtuse. A dog is a dog even if a former soul does inhabit it."

Miss Sanderson carefully set her cup down. "Do you still have the dog?"

"No," Sybil told her. "She got old and quite smelly and I had her put down. Now, Mr. Forsythe, I was explaining my theories—"

"Dangerous ones. If what you think is true none of us are responsible for our own actions. Does that include murder?"

"It would have to. Let's consider it this way. Some are born to be victims, others born to be aggressors. The aggressors prey upon the victims."

"In that case, where do you place Katherine St. Croix?"

"Aha!" Cocking her head, Sybil winked a bright eye. "There *is* a oneness! You and I were once owls. I was your mate, of course. The wisdom carries over. Now, your shrewd question. Katherine was both. For a time she was an aggressor; then another stronger aggressor came along and made her the victim. It was nice to hear she was dead but we're not rid of her. Katherine is now a serpent and crawls upon her belly." Snapping her fan closed, Sybil aimed it at her sister. "If you see a snake in the woods or the garden, Bella, you must kill it."

"I couldn't, Sis."

"Then you may find Katherine in your bed. Silly girl!"

Forsythe darted a look of sheer frustration at his secretary, who grinned back. "How well did you know Miss St. Croix?"

"Hardly at all. Bella picked up pieces of gossip about the woman from Mrs. Larkin. I never set foot in my brother's house but Bella sneaks into the kitchen to take them casseroles and pies and cakes. I've told you over and over not to go to the Priory and not to waste our food on that brother of ours."

Bella flushed. "Not just Amyas I'm thinking of, Sis.

There's Cassie and Carl. Mrs. Larkin is not a good cook, you know."

"Mrs. Larkin is a *terrible* cook. And an awful house-keeper. Just what Amyas deserves. He's such a fool. Keeping a servant around who spends all her time painting her nails."

"The house looks awful, Sis—floors not washed and dust all over the place."

"Good! A pig sty for a pig. Yes, Bella, in his next incarnation Amyas will be either a pig or a jackass. I can't decide which."

"Miss Sybil," Forsythe said. "Cassandra tells us you moved out of the Priory shortly before the death of your sister-in-law."

"Indeed we did. Divorce, Mr. Forsythe. Amyas had been trying to persuade my sister-in-law to divorce him for years. He said they weren't happy, but I assure you neither Amyas nor Viola would have been happy with anyone else. As I told him, why not stay together and not ruin two houses. I've never liked Amyas and I couldn't bear Viola but—"

"I liked Viola," Bella said timidly. "She was so pretty."

"Your taste is strictly in your mouth. Mr. Forsythe, if Jack the Ripper came to the door my sister would not only serve him tea and biscuits but offer to sharpen his knife."

"The quarrel with your brother," Forsythe reminded.

"The last straw was when I heard my brother bribing Viola to set him free. He offered her any amount she wanted if she would divorce him. I was outraged. Never, in any incarnation, have Dancers divorced. I beseeched him to change his mind and he told me to mind my own business. I told him I could no longer stay under his roof, so Bella and I came here. Since that moment I have not spoken a word to him. Viola dropped in once in a while and I could tell Amyas and that Proctor man were swaying her. I urged her to remember her vows and her duty but she refused to listen and that is why she died."

"Why did she die?" asked a bewildered Miss Sanderson.

"Destiny. Viola was destined to remain my brother's wife. When she tried to forsake her sacred vows, fate struck her down. The night of her birthday dinner I knew she was to die. Bella and I had been invited but—"

"I *wanted* to go, Sis."

"Hold your tongue. You jabber incessantly. After dinner, Mr. Forsythe, Viola came to this house attired in a ridiculous costume. A sailor suit! I took one look and told her she resembled Popeye the Sailor and she got quite haughty. I asked her whether she had decided to divorce and she told me she intended to do what *she* wished. I warned her. I said, 'Viola, that way lies destruction.' She laughed at me. I told her she was a foolish vain creature and would come back to this world as a peacock—"

"Peahen, Sis. A female is always called—"

"Peacock, Bella. Spreading her tail and looking for admiration. David Proctor will be a peacock also. Egotistical chap."

Forsythe was rubbing his brow. "And fate struck Lady Dancer down."

"The moment that Carl came running over to tell us his mother's bed hadn't been slept in and they couldn't find her I knew she was dead. Bella insisted on joining the searchers and I like a nice stroll so I went along. We were looking in the woods when we heard Horace shouting from the direction of the China Sea. We got down there just in time to see Carl dragging Viola's body out of the water. The boy had stripped right down to his undershorts and was shivering. I told him to get some clothes on and then I had to look after Horace. The poor man was going berserk and no one could understand what he wanted. It was that sailor outfit. Horace didn't want his daughter to meet her maker in that garb. I had Mrs. Larkin hold blankets and Bella and I disrobed Viola and put her into a dressing gown. When Horace got the sailor clothes he was content and ran into the woods to hide them." Sybil paused to catch her breath and then said graciously, "In a matter of days, Mr. Forsythe, it will be a year since Viola's death. You must come to the celebration Horace is planning—"

"Celebration," Forsythe echoed weakly.

"Call it a memorial service. It sounds like fun. Horace is planning on having all of us throw flowers into the lake—he can't buy them because he has no money, but I believe Cassandra is providing them—and there'll be music and that sort of thing. He's holding it rather late unfortunately. Viola was over here shortly after ten and we assume she must have drowned soon after she left, so Horace has set the time at midnight. Do come!" She added offhandedly, "You may bring your secretary if you wish."

"Thanks a heap," Miss Sanderson mumbled.

"You're quite welcome," Sybil told her politely and then proceeded to ignore her again. "I suppose, Mr. Forsythe, you would like to hear about Katherine St. Croix."

Forsythe breathed an audible sigh of relief. "That is why Miss Sanderson and I are here."

"I think in your next incarnation you will be a . . . yes, a bloodhound. I shall be a hummingbird, darting around from flower to flower. We may meet."

"We may. Miss Sybil, Katherine St. Croix."

"An unpleasant creature. As I said Mrs. Larkin gossiped on and on to Bella about the woman. Told her Katherine was making a dead set for Amyas. I rather wish he *had* married the woman. Serve him right. But then Katherine had the audacity to come here. Pretended she wanted to know if I had mementos from the family that she could look at. As a matter of fact I have a trunk in the attic simply stuffed with letters and photographs, but I wouldn't let her see them. I took one look at her and saw she had a bad aura—her head was ringed with black—and I thought, if you were in my house, my girl, I'd lock up the silver."

"What day was she here?" Forsythe asked.

92

"I've no idea. Bella?"

"It was Wednesday, Sis. I always walk into Harper on Wednesdays to pick up the meat and groceries and when I got back—"

"That's correct. You got home just as I was admitting Katherine. I sent you to the kitchen to put the food away and brought the woman in here. I didn't waste any time with her. I told her if my brother was mad enough to let a person of her type into his house that was his business, but I wouldn't have her in mine. Then I showed her the door. She didn't come back."

Bella, who had been stuffing cheese puffs into her mouth, sputtered and her sister said sharply, "Don't talk with your mouth full and do wipe the crumbs off your chin. Now, what are you trying to say?"

Bella swallowed, wiped off her chin, and blurted, "That wasn't all, Sis. Katherine asked you a lot of questions. She wanted to know when Cassie had gotten back from the States and where her commune was located. She asked when David Proctor had come to Harper and where he'd lived before that. Then she asked about Horace's wife, when she died and how. She asked you why Carl hadn't continued with his rock group and—"

"That's right," her sister interrupted. "I'll admit I forgot that."

Forsythe was frowning. "Did you answer these questions?"

The turban shook violently. "I told the woman if she wanted questions answered she could go elsewhere. I assured her my brother might be hoodwinked into thinking that butter wouldn't melt in her mouth, but I could see her for what she was. By the time she left she was so angry her aura had turned to deep red and—" Stopping abruptly, Sybil wheeled on her sister, snapped the fan shut, and struck Bella's wrist sharply. "How do you know what we said? You were in the kitchen all the time she was here."

93

"I was listening at the door, Sis. That's the only way I find anything out."

"Sneaky, nasty, and sly. Full of too much curiosity. Arabella Dancer, in your next life you will be an alley cat. You'll be cold and bony and find your food in rubbish bins!"

Bella cowered back and tugged distractedly at her braid. "Don't say that, Sis. Please!"

Miss Sanderson took pity. She patted the older woman's broad shoulder. "I'm sure you'll be a house cat, Miss Bella. Much loved and you'll sleep on a pillow and drink cream."

"An alley cat!" Sybil divided a hostile glance between her sister and Miss Sanderson. The beady eyes shifted to Forsythe and she gave him a sweet smile. "Any further questions, Mr. Forsythe?"

Thankfully he got to his feet. "That about covers it. Thank you. Oh, could you direct us to the ruins? We'd like to meet Horace Gillimede."

In a rustle of satin, Sybil came to her feet. "You could circle the woods, but that's a long walk. There's a shortcut through the woods. Better take that."

"Sis, the woods are full of bogs and sinkholes." Bella gave Miss Sanderson a shy smile. "I'm taking some goodies over to Horace. I'll show you the way."

Sybil sighed heavily. "More food for Horace. Oh well, I don't mind. He's not a bad old chap. Bella not only cooks things for him but plants a kitchen garden twice the size we need so Horace can steal from it. I won't have him in the house though. He smells even worse than mother did."

"She means the dog," Bella confided.

"They know whom I mean. Run along, Bella, and get your basket and don't go near the Priory. Be sure to take good care of Mr. Forsythe. I shouldn't want him to meet his end in a bog." Putting a possessive hand on Forsythe's arm, she led him to the door. Miss Sanderson trailed along behind. "Drop in any time, Mr. Forsythe. It's so pleasant to meet another Seeing Soul. If we don't meet again in this life we certainly will in another."

They stopped to wait for their guide and Miss Sanderson glanced back at the stone cottage. "Seems you're at the top of the Seeing Souls' hit parade, Robby."

"Rather looks that way."

"Miss Sybil wouldn't give a hoot whether *I* fell into a bog."

"Your aura must not be right."

"Did you notice she left me out of her predictions? I wonder what I will be in my next life?"

He stroked his chin. "Let's see . . ."

"Perhaps a butterfly?"

"Doesn't seem to fit. You have a remarkable memory. Sandy, how would you like to be an elephant?"

"How would you like a smack across the mouth?"

"Temper! Your aura is turning red."

"And yours—Here's Bella."

Bella had donned a wide-brimmed straw hat and carried baskets over both arms. "Keep right behind me," she ordered, and plunged into the woods.

Abigail Sanderson and Robert Forsythe plunged in behind her.

CHAPTER EIGHT

Bella Dancer was the first to trot out of the shadows of the trees into the sunlit glade. She pulled to a stop and her companions slowly came into view behind her. Miss Sanderson paused to catch her breath. "Robby, it would seem all Dancers either race through tangled underbrush or clamber up flights of stairs." She detached several dried leaves from her hair and pulled a burr from her linen skirt.

He mopped at a hot brow. "They do seem to move like locomotives. Pleasant spot."

The glade where the ruin of the Priory was located was sylvan. Parts of the building still stood and around them gray stones were scattered as if a giant child had petulantly knocked over a stack of blocks. Vines coiled around the stones and wild flowers grew profusely up through the turf. Bella strolled back toward them and held out a wicker basket to Forsythe. It was covered with a linen cloth. "Give this to Horace. He'll be around somewhere. I must take this other one over to Mrs. Larkin."

Smoothing back her rumpled gray hair, Miss Sanderson said, "Your sister said you weren't to go to the Priory."

"What Sis doesn't know won't hurt her." Bella straightened the straw hat and tugged at her braid. "Miss Sanderson . . ."

"Yes."

Bella's wide mouth moved convulsively and then she blurted, "Cats *eat* birds!"

Clutching the basket destined for Mrs. Larkin, Bella fled back into the woods. Looking after her, Miss Sanderson said solemnly, "Indeed they do."

"Let's beard the goat in his lair."

"I hardly think goats live in lairs, Robby."

They walked slowly toward the ruins. As they drew closer they could see that one block, overgrown with vines, had an iron stovepipe sticking rakishly from a tin roof. The only opening, a low doorway, was covered with what looked like burlap sacking. As they approached the sack was thrust aside and a tall man emerged, bending his head to clear the lintel. Miss Sanderson stopped abruptly and gripped her companion's arm. "Robby." She moaned.

"He's not the man we saw in Bury-Sutton. Take a closer look, Sandy."

She took a closer look and then gave a deep sigh of relief. "No, he isn't. He's taller and his shoulders are wider. But at first glance he . . ." She gave a shaky laugh. "I'm acting like a fool. I had a nightmare, you know. We were sitting in that church and staring at that coffin covered with orchids and that bearded man was howling like a wolf outside and . . ."

"It's over, Sandy. Come."

They walked to meet Horace Gillimede. As they drew closer Forsythe realized what a size the man was. He towered over both of them; his shoulders were immensely wide, his chest the size and shape of a barrel. He wore a single garment, obviously made of burlap sacks, reaching to his knees. A chunk of rope girded it and he was shod in leather sandals with thongs laced to his calves. Long matted hair fell to his shoulders and an equally matted beard touched the rope at his waist. His voice was deep, rich, and clear. "You come looking for a killer and you have found one."

"We come looking for Horace Gillimede," Forsythe told him.

"And a killer. My son-in-law told me of you. I know who you are and whence you came." He darted a look at the wicker basket.

Forsythe proffered it. "Miss Bella sent this for you."

"A good woman. Come into my humble abode and I will give you refreshment."

Miss Sanderson shook her head violently and Forsythe, who had also caught the stench wafting from the old man, said hastily, "Too nice a day to be inside. And we had rather a lot of refreshment at the Misses Dancer, Mr. Gillimede."

"You must call me Horace. I do not use titles. What are your given names?"

Forsythe told him and the man bobbed his unkempt head. "Abigail and Robert. We will sit over here. There is some shade."

The spot he indicated was not only in the shade cast by a tall crumbling wall but also had three widely spaced flat stones. Miss Sanderson selected the stone farthest from their host and perched on it. Looking from one to the other, Horace repeated, "You have found a *killer*."

"I don't think you're confessing to the murder of Katherine St. Croix."

"No. I speak of my wife who was wayward and fell into mortal sin. Her sins I shouldered, as I should have had thought more of her, but instead spent my days grubbing for the Devil's tool—money. I drove my erring wife and her lover from my house and they perished. Even this—" He waved a huge hand. "This is too good for me. I am the lowest of the low. But the good Lord is merciful and He allows me to atone."

Piercing gray eyes moved from Forsythe to his secretary. "I came, after I had rid myself of the Devil's tool, to watch over my daughter. Viola was a lamb washed by God and for a time she was sinless. Then she fell into the sins of the flesh and was tempted by another man. She sought to forsake her vows and commit adultery. But, as I said, the good Lord is merciful and He reached down and plucked her up to His bosom while still her soul was pure."

"Lady Dancer drowned," Miss Sanderson murmured.

"The waves rolled over her. When we searched for Viola I went immediately to the lake. I knew it was there I would find my child." Horace stared down at his knotted fists and his voice changed. "She was always afraid of water. When she was a tiny child I tried to rid her of that fear. I'd take her into the pool and tell her, 'darling, there is nothing to be afraid of.' Viola would cling to me and scream. She was such a pretty little thing and she grew into a beautiful woman. How terrified she must have been when she died. Daddy wasn't there to save her. I feel . . . I feel she must have called out to me. I dived into the lake to find her but it was Carleton who touched her arm and drew her out on the bank. She wore the same blasphemous clothes she had worn the evening before. Trousers! In all her life Viola had never worn trousers. I never cared for them and when Viola was small and begged for the overalls her playmates wore, I wouldn't allow them. I'd tell my wife, dress my daughter as a *girl*."

"The sailor outfit upset you?" Forsythe asked.

"I couldn't bear to see her in it, Robert. Of all the people gathered around my daughter's body only Sybil understood. She clothed my child in a robe and gave those Devil's garments to me."

"What did you do with them?"

"Cut them into pieces and burned them. There." He jerked his head toward the stone hut. "I've made a petrol drum into a rude stove and I consigned them to its flames.

99

Then I spoke of them no more. But I tell you now, as the Lord may direct your search. You look for the hand that slew Katherine St. Croix."

"We do. Can you help us?"

"The woman sought me out. First she spoke of the Dancer history, but I could tell her little. She asked about the family, but I had no answers. Time and tide make little difference to me. I have forsaken the world. My granddaughter came to me and warned me against the woman, but I told Cassandra the woman had asked me to wrestle the devil in her soul. I could not turn her away."

Miss Sanderson was looking rather helplessly at her employer and finally he said, "Do you remember the questions Miss St. Croix asked?"

Under the tangled hair the broad and rather noble brow furrowed. "I cannot. They were questions of a temporal nature and as such held no interest. I would answer if I could. I can tell you little about the woman. She was fair to look upon, but we mustn't let beauty blind us. Jezebel and Delilah were also fair."

The old man fell silent, perhaps considering the danger of feminine beauty. "There was evil in the woman but some good. She confessed she was a sinner but said she had taken to sin because she was an orphan and had been raised in poverty. The woman said she might find her salvation here." He lifted his head and a gleam of shrewdness crossed his massive features. "I have not quite lost all connection with the world and I knew what she was hinting at. She had hoped to become my son-in-law's wife. I warned Katherine that Amyas is a man without sensitivity or consideration. I told her I had given Viola in her tender youth into this man's hands and he had cast her aside for scarlet women. I recounted my own sins and she commiserated with me. There were tears in her eyes as we spoke of my poor dead wife and she told me she understood why the shock had been so great when my daughter went to her judgment clad in men's attire. She begged me to intercede on her behalf with my granddaughter as she felt Cassandra was against her." The huge shoulders moved. "I can tell you no more."

Forsythe shifted on the rock. "Do you remember the night of Miss St. Croix's death?"

"No. As I have told you time is not important to me. I live, I forage in the woods for my sustenance. The Lord provides mushrooms and berries and roots. I eat neither the flesh of animal nor fowl nor fish. I cut dead trees to provide fuel for my stove and I walk the land and look upon the miracles the Lord has created for man."

"Could you have been walking the night that she died?"

"I walk every night, Robert, upon the fields and through the woods. I roam along the banks of the lake and sometimes when the night is windy I hear my daughter calling to me. 'Daddy,' Viola calls, 'Daddy, save me!'" A hand wrenched violently at his hair as though he would pull it from his scalp. Miss Sanderson made an involuntary sound and his hand fell away. He gave her a reassuring smile of great sweetness. "Be calm, my child. I have frightened you. It's only that memory tears at my heart. The evening of Viola's birthday I was severe with her. I did not speak of her costume while we were at the table. I ate nothing as I have sworn never to let food from my son-in-law's table pass my lips. But I watched my daughter, flaunting her body, and I thought, my wayward lamb, you go the way your mother trod before you. After the dinner, when I walked with her over to the Dower House, I reasoned with her and Viola laughed and called me foolish. She reminded me I had put her into Amyas' hands and I could not refute this. She reminded me she had been only seventeen at that time but now she was old enough to make her own decisions. Always when we parted she kissed my cheek. This night she did not. Viola was hot with anger and flew from my side and entered the house where I could not follow. So I walked the land and prayed for her soul."

Forsythe looked at his bowed head and got slowly to his feet. Miss Sanderson shut off her snooper and followed his example. "Thank you, Horace," the barrister said gently. "Can you direct us back to the road?"

"Please, not through the woods," Miss Sanderson said.

"I will take you." Horace pulled himself to his feet. "You must watch your footing. The land is rough."

Horace not only smelled remarkably like a goat but he moved like one, fairly bounding over the turf. At a slower pace, the other two followed. "The poor old fellow," Miss Sanderson muttered. "But a complete waste of our time."

"Looks that way. But one never knows. Tired?"

"Exhausted. I wish now I'd let you bring the car." She looked up at him. "We're not doing any more interviews today I hope."

"Nary a one. Too late. The sun is going down."

"I'll be heartily glad to get back to the snuggery and a cold glass of brew."

They walked on. The land dipped and they lost sight of their guide's prancing figure. As they climbed the other sloping side Miss Sanderson stumbled and swore heartily. Forsythe grabbed her arm. "Careful, Sandy. Holes all over the place."

"And I just stepped into one and twisted my ankle. Thank God, there's the road."

"And the gateposts. Ah, Horace is bidding us goodbye."

He stopped, turned back toward them, and raised a bare arm. Sunset cast a golden glow over his beard and face. "Your road lies that way. God go with you!"

"He'll have to." Miss Sanderson stooped to rub her ankle. "Robby, I don't think I can walk any farther. My ankle hurts like hell!"

He sank to a knee and touched her leg gently. "You've done a job on it. Swelling up like a balloon. Lean on me."

She hobbled along, leaning heavily on his arm. When

102

they reached the ditch she sank down with a groan. "Sorry, Robby, guess this is as far as I go."

He looked around. "I don't like to leave you here, Sandy."

"You'll have to. Go and get the car. I'll be fine."

He didn't argue and simply strode off down the road. She shivered and buttoned up her jacket. The air was becoming fresh and the breeze was cool. Long shadows fell over her from the hedgerow. Exercise! she thought wrathfully. Not only did her ankle ache but so did her head. Wearily she pillowed her face on her arms. Then she started and jerked her head up. A shadow not from the hedgerow darkened her face.

"What in hell are you doing down there?"

She recognized the voice and said sharply, "Why did you sneak up like that, Mr. Proctor?"

"Sorry. Didn't mean to give you a start. I saw this huddled thing by the hedge and thought it might be an animal."

"A wounded animal. Twisted my ruddy ankle and Robby's gone for the car. Where's your bike?"

"Old Faithful blew another tire and I had to walk out here today. Flaming nuisance, that bike. I'll be glad when I have a car."

"Perhaps Cassandra will give you one for a wedding present," Miss Sanderson said tartly.

"You must be psychic. That's what she promised." Proctor added smugly, "A Jaguar, to be exact."

"Quite suitable."

"Yes. Like me to hang around until Mr. Forsythe gets back?"

No time for false pride, she thought. She didn't like the man but any company was better than sitting helplessly in the dark. She gestured hospitably, "Draw up a chair."

He sank lithely down at her side and touched her swollen ankle. "Hurt?"

She winced. "You could say so."

"Detecting can be dangerous work. How is the investigation coming?"

"I've no idea. Robby's the brain; I'm only the hired help."

He flipped back the lock of hair from his brow. "You forgot the book of poems yesterday."

"Completely."

"I have it here. Was going to drop it off at the inn tonight." He tugged the thin book out of a gray flannel pocket and gave it to her with a charming smile. "Tell me what you think of my work."

She nodded and tucked it into her handbag. "Our charger arrives. Care for a lift?"

"Delighted. I'll return the compliment when I get my Jaguar."

"Will that be soon?"

"Hopefully. Cass proposed again today and I accepted." He added righteously, "In a few days Viola will have been dead for a year."

The headlights from the Rover glared in their faces, blinding them. With the young man's assistance Forsythe lifted his secretary into the car. With Proctor in the back seat they headed back toward Harper.

CHAPTER NINE

Forsythe pulled the Rover up in front of the Widow Hawkins' narrow brick house and deposited David Proctor. Proctor stuck his head in the window. "If you need any help with Miss Sanderson . . ."

"Everything in hand," Forsythe told him.

"I'll bet," Miss Sanderson said glumly as they rolled past Miss Pyne's house and made the turn beside the church. "I'll never be able to get up those steep stairs."

"Wait and see."

At the Harper Arms she found a cluster of people waiting. Matthew Bantam, flanked by two husky barmaids, came to meet them, followed by old Bob hobbling along on a stout cane. Mr. Bantam gave orders like a top sergeant. "Annie, you get back to the bar. Nell, come along with us. Bob, get out of the way. Now, Mr. Forsythe, we'll make a seat with our hands. That's the way. Up we go, Miss Sanderson. Bob, let go of the lass' leg!"

Perching comfortably astride Bantam's balloon of a stomach, Miss Sanderson was borne up to the first floor and deposited on her bed. Disregarding the landlord's orders old Bob peered in from the doorway. "Out you go, Bob! You

105

come along too, Mr. Forsythe. Nell can get Miss Sanderson ready for the doctor, can't you, girl?"

"That I can, sir. Stripped down my mum many the time when she was blind drunk."

"I," Miss Sanderson announced with what dignity she could muster, "am not blind drunk."

Shooing the barrister and old Bob before him, Bantam made a stately departure. As soon as Miss Sanderson had been completely stripped and clad in pajamas, pillows piled behind her shoulders and under her injured leg, the doctor came into the room. He was a young man with bristling red hair and an ill-tempered expression. "Let's have a look," he grunted, and proceeded to pull and tug at the injured leg. Miss Sanderson bit down hard on her lower lip and tears of pain sprang to her eyes. Dropping the leg back on the pillow, he straightened, fished in his bag, and slapped down a vial of white capsules. "You're lucky. No bones broken. Nell, get some towels and ice and apply cold compresses. When the swelling goes down I'll put an elastic bandage on it. Get two of these pills into Miss . . ."

"Sanderson," Forsythe supplied. He'd returned and was leaning against the door frame.

"Two pills every four hours." He glared down at the patient. "Stay off that leg for at least forty-eight hours—"

"I can't," Miss Sanderson wailed. "I've work to do."

"Forty-eight hours now or a couple of weeks later if you put weight on that sprain. Suit yourself. Makes no difference to me." Snapping the bag shut, he shoved past Forsythe.

"Well!" Color flared in the secretary's face. "Fine bedside manner!"

Forsythe grinned. "Doctor Beam knows his business and that's the main thing. Follow doctor's orders and I'll bring supper up and we'll dine together."

The pills and the cold compresses helped and by the time Forsythe reappeared with a loaded tray Miss Sanderson was in a better mood. The barrister noticed the mishap hadn't diminished her appetite. Only after she had finished did she comment on the daisies stuck into a jar on the tray. "Your contribution?"

"Old Bob's. Probably a thank you for the neat feeling up he gave your leg."

She laughed. "He's an opportunist, right enough. But, Robby, stuck here for two days while you race around interviewing? How will you get along without the snooper? You can't carry the handbag and thrust it at people."

"It would look a trifle odd. I'll have to play it by ear, Sandy, and trust to memory."

She snorted. "Lots of luck! But there's only Mrs. Larkin and George left."

"I'm not looking forward to either of them. I've a hunch they won't prove to be my favorite people." Forsythe sighed. "Tomorrow afternoon I'll tackle them."

"Cheer up," she told him. "They can't possibly be worse than the Dancers."

The next day proved to be the hottest and the sultriest thus far that season. Forsythe settled for casual slacks and an open-necked shirt. When he pulled the Rover to a stop before the Priory he took a moment to roll his shirt sleeves above the elbows. As he stepped out into the heat he spotted one of the people he wanted to interview close at hand. George was lazily and ineffectually scything tall grass near the drive. Mouse-colored hair fell forward over a low brow and his face glistened with sweat. He stopped his desultory motions, wiped a shirt sleeve across his face, and stared. In the snake-like throat the lump of Adam's apple bobbed unpleasantly.

"I want to talk with you," Forsythe said curtly and waded through the grass toward him.

"And I know why. Sir Amyas told me to tell you what I told the police a dozen times. Here goes." He leaned on the scythe and spoke rapidly. "Didn't see the St. Croix woman arrive and didn't see her leave. Got no alibi the night she was done in. Was driving around in my sister's car and didn't stop no place. No use checking for a police record. Only black mark against me is car theft and I was just a kid at the time. Sister's clean. Not even a parking ticket. Clarks may not be gentry but they're honest. Anything else?"

Forsythe stopped and looked the man over. George Clark still wore black trousers, now covered with grass seeds, but had exchanged his white jacket for a cotton shirt. He was lanky and had shifty eyes. Hardly prepossessing, the barrister thought. "Like to enlarge on that a bit?" Forsythe asked.

"Told you everything."

"Hardly. How long have you been in service here?"

" 'Bout five and a half years."

"How do you like it?"

"Pretty dull place but Maggie and me been in worse. Lotta work but the old man don't bother us none."

"Are you speaking about Sir Amyas?"

"Sure am. Not a bad bloke. Always in cloud cuckoo land but he pays good."

"Before you came here—were you in service?"

"Maggie and me been in service since I was—guess I was about eighteen. This is the best job we've had." George became more expansive. "Can hit some rough places. 'Fore we came here we worked for a family in Leeds. Slavedrivers! That's where Maggie—sister wants me to call her Margaret now but she's still Maggie to me— anyway, where Maggie met her Ned. Hear her talk about Ned Larkin you'd think he was the second coming but he was no good. Smooth talker but hit the bottle something fierce. One night old Ned wrapped himself around a bottle of gin and tried to drive a Bentley through a stone wall. Maggie was glad to get rid of him. Maggie gives herself airs. Our old mum used to tell her, 'girl, better remember your station in life. Don't go breaking your heart for what you can't have.' Think Maggie listened? Not on your life. Pored over those fashion magazines learning to dress proper and took a course in how to talk. Has her heart set on getting Sir Amyas."

Forsythe cocked his head. "I shouldn't imagine you'd object to being Sir Amyas' brother-in-law."

The shifty eyes turned dreamily to the Elizabethan house. "Bet your bottom on that. Sit in a big chair smoking cigars and drinking brandy and watch someone else work. But mum was right and Maggie's just pipe dreaming. Got as much chance of pinning the old man as I have in walking a tightrope. After Lady Dancer died Maggie got pretty hopeful. Swarmed all over the old man like a hen with one chick. Didn't do her no good. Sir Amyas couldn't see her for dust and if he was gonna get married he would have taken that St. Croix bird."

"Do you think Katherine St. Croix had a chance of becoming Lady Dancer?"

"She was a shoo-in before Miss Cassandra got the dirt on her and turfed her out. Had the old man breathing fire. Could give you my opinion of the woman in one word not usually heard in mixed company." George Clark eyed the barrister and apparently decided against the word. "She was the kind of bird got a bloke all steamy wriggling her tail at him and then cooled him off in one hell of a hurry. Tell you the truth I don't think she *liked* men."

Forsythe was uncomfortable. He could feel sweat gathering in the small of his back and trickling down. Taking out a handkerchief he wiped at his face. "The Sunday that Miss St. Croix disappeared—did you see her that day?"

"Had me running my legs off all day. My bunion was giving me trouble and I was up and down those stairs taking her trays any number of times. Started at lunch time. Took up her lunch and later coffee and then her dinner tray."

"What was she doing?"

"Sprawling on a lounge thing, taking her ease. Said she was sick but she sure didn't look it. Cleaned up every scrap on her trays too."

"Did she talk to you?"

"Gimme orders is all. Do this, draw the shades, put the tray down over there. Sure high and mighty for a sneak thief!"

"Of course, at the time you had no idea about her past."

"Didn't know nothing about it 'til Sir Amyas found her rotting down at Mandalay. Didn't break my heart when he found her body, but she *was* a good-looking bird."

Sliding the handkerchief down his shirt, Forsythe dabbed at his wet chest. "This alibi you mentioned. You say you drove around that Sunday evening."

"Left the house as soon as dinner was done. Maggie cooks dinner and then charges in to eat with the family and play lady of the manor while I serve. After they eat Maggie leaves it to me to clean up. That night I stuck the dishes in the washing-up machine and dabbed at the kitchen a bit. Then I went into our sitting room and asked Maggie for the keys to her car. She's got an old Morris Minor. Left the house around ten and drove around. Fine night it was. Warm and balmy."

"Any particular direction?"

George waved a hand. "Over toward Chester. Took a bunch of back roads just to put in time. This place is dull enough at the best of times but on Sunday it dies. Came back here after one—"

"That was rather a long time to drive aimlessly around."

"That's my story," George said pugnaciously.

I'd better get out of this sun before I melt, Forsythe thought. He took a couple of steps toward the house and then spun around. "To your knowledge did Miss St. Croix leave her room that day?"

"Nah. Just lay there like a pussy full of cream ordering me around. Mr. Carleton said she went down to his suite—

he's on the second floor—and picked up the money for them buttons, but I didn't see her go." The man wiped both hands down his pant legs and then blurted, "Hey, clean forgot! She *did* go outta that room. I had to take some towels up to the bathrooms—"

"What time?"

"Let's see . . . must've been a little before two. Yeah, that's right. Always have a cuppa with Maggie at two and I was thinking of that when I went up with the towels. The woman's door was open and I looked in and she wasn't there. Wondered where she'd gotten to. Figured she might be in the bathroom but she wasn't. Then I noticed the door of this little room they call a writing room was closed. Never seen anyone writing in there and the door's always open. So I open it and walk in. The St. Croix woman was sitting at the desk using the telephone. She looks up and bangs the receiver down and gives me hell. Tells me I'm an eavesdropper and I tell her if I was I wouldn't have opened the door; I would have my ear glued to it. She walks past me, goes into her room, and slams the door."

"Did you hear any of the conversation?"

"No. Like I said she banged the receiver down when she seen me."

"Could she have been speaking with someone in the house?"

"Sure could have. They put phones in where all you got to do is press the right button to get the library and study and kitchen. Phones up in Miss Cassandra's attic and in Mr. Carleton's rooms too. But she could have been using an outside line too."

"I see." Forsythe looked searchingly at the older man. "That drive you took . . . did you pick up a passenger at the Harper Arms?"

George swore lustily. "I suppose that bird has been talking a blue streak! Yeah, I took Nell for a ride. Trust a bird to talk!"

111

Forsythe grinned. "As a matter of fact Nell hasn't said a word."

"How'd you know then?"

"Mr. Bantam mentioned you'd told Nell about Miss Sanderson and me. And you don't seem the type to drive around alone."

"You caught me out. Nell and me plan to get married. She's not a bad sort of girl."

Too good for you, Forsythe decided silently. Aloud he said, "Why didn't you tell the police?"

"Maggie. If my sister finds out I'm courting a maid the fur is going to fly." The lump in his throat moved convulsively. "You gonna tell Maggie?"

"I see no reason to. It will be our secret. Where can I find your sister?"

George peered at his watch. "Maggie will be in our sitting room. Walk right in and down the hall toward the kitchen. Take a right turn where the hall branches." He glanced up. "Take it easy on the old girl. Maggie's as much in cloud cuckoo land as Sir Amyas is." He added glumly, "She'll be coming down to earth soon enough anyway."

Despite the domestic shortage, Forsythe thought, the Dancers had scraped the bottom of the barrel with George Clark. His sister proved to have acquired a smoother veneer. She welcomed the barrister to her sitting room with all the panache of a seasoned hostess, seated him, and pressed a tall, frosty, and welcome glass of iced tea into his hand. Forsythe scrutinized the room and Margaret Larkin. The room was comfortable and, unlike the rest of the house, immaculately clean. A large color television and a stereo dominated it. Mrs. Larkin was a Junoesque woman, her ample curves expertly and probably expensively corseted into an hourglass shape. Her legs were a touch heavy but shapely and her Italian sandals had four-inch heels. This housekeeper didn't stoop to a uniform but wore a white silk dress ornamented with thin gold chains. She waved a well-

112

kept hand with long painted nails. "This suite belonged to Sybil and Bella but when they moved Sir Amyas suggested George and I might be more comfortable down here. I do miss the dear aunts. Bella did all the cooking and a great deal of the cleaning. She's very good at both."

She spoke of the Misses Dancer as though they were servants for whom she might be giving a recommendation. "They seem quite comfortable in the Dower House," he told her.

"Sybil may be but Bella hungers to be back here. She has boundless *energy*. Bella tells me you met Horace yesterday. Dear old chap but a little . . . well, peculiar. When his daughter died he seemed to go quite strange. Carried a Bible around and made us swear on it never to reveal about the clothes dear Lady Dancer was wearing when she drowned. I couldn't quite understand it. Horace seemed more disturbed by that than by his daughter's death."

Forsythe took another cool delicious sip from the frosted glass. "Your brother tells me you've been here for a number of years."

"So long it seems like home to us. Oddly enough neither of us really welcomed the idea of burying ourselves in the country. But we had to come. Lady Dancer simply couldn't find anyone willing to help out and, as I always say, blood is thicker than water."

"You're related to the family?"

She bent her head and treated him to the sight of a straight white part in the midst of glossy black hair. "Distantly connected—on our mother's side."

The old mum, Forsythe mused, who had warned this woman not to aspire above her station. "Miss St. Croix's death must have been a shock to you."

"I was stunned. Many people in our position would have left the Priory immediately. The scandal, you know. But George and I feel we must stand by the family in their hour of need."

"Most commendable, Mrs. Larkin. Miss Dancer mentioned you distrusted Miss St. Croix."

"At sight. A perfectly horrible woman! Set Sir Amyas and his son at each other's throats. Deplorable."

"You were here the night of her death?"

"Yes. I seldom leave the estate except for an occasional visit to Chester." Polished nails touched the black hair. "Mainly to have my hair done. One must look after one's appearance."

Definitely genteel, Forsythe thought. Speaking with careful and slow diction. "Could you tell me how you spent the evening?"

"Right here. As soon as dinner was finished I came in to watch a couple of programs on television. Educational, of course. I do so deplore most of the trashy shows the public is forced to watch. I retired about eleven and read for about an hour. The police asked whether I had heard Miss St. Croix leave the house and I told them no. The Dancers are amazing people, so talented and exciting, but I fear they're a wee bit lax when it comes to locking up. As I tell George we could all be murdered in our sleep and none the wiser."

They're a wee bit lax when it comes to servants too, Forsythe decided as he put down his glass and rose. "One last question, Mrs. Larkin. A hundred pounds were found in Miss St. Croix's carryall. Could she have stolen the money from you?"

"Heavens no, Mr. Forsythe. Dear Sir Amyas insists we keep our funds in his safe. Such a considerate, thoughtful man he is."

That's not what I've heard, Forsythe thought as he thanked her and took his departure. He retraced his steps to the hall in time to see Cassandra, her arm linked with David Proctor's, skipping down the stairs. She wore a pastel pink jogging suit and the material between her breasts was darkened with a sweat stain. She dragged her close-set eyes from Proctor's handsome face and said with no evidence of delight, "Oh, it's you again. David tells me your friend had an accident."

"Twisted her ankle. I've just come from Mrs. Larkin. Can you give me one good reason why you keep that pair on here?"

Proctor looked at a dust smudge on his hand and echoed the words. "One good reason, Cass."

She giggled. "Inertia. They're fixtures now. And they weren't always so slack. When mother was alive and the aunts were here the Lark and George boy earned their salaries. Now they act as though work was a four-letter word. But Amy hates change and Carl wouldn't notice if he was wading through garbage." She beamed up at Proctor. "Good news, Mr. Forsythe. David has finally decided to let me make an honest man of him. We're going to be married very soon."

"Congratulations." Forsythe shook the younger man's hand. As he did he noticed a slender gold band on the poet's wrist. "Patek. Did the police locate your stolen watch?"

"Hardly. Didn't bother reporting the theft. No use. They never find anything anyway. This is a wedding present."

"When will you be married?"

Cassandra twirled away from them, coming lightly to her toes. For a moment Forsythe thought she was going to do knee bends but she ended up possessively grasping her fiance's arm—a bare arm with dark hair curling down to the wrist, Forsythe noted. Proctor had forsaken his shabby flannels and wore designer jeans and a scarlet polo shirt. Perhaps more wedding presents. The girl squeezed the bare arm and smiled dazzlingly. "Soon. On Saturday mother will have been dead for a year. David says any time after that. We'll have a quiet service and then take off for a tour of the Continent. When we return we'll select a house."

"You don't plan to stay on here?" Forsythe asked.

Proctor shook his head. "Cass and I have had enough of the Priory and Harper. We're thinking of Belgravia. I think I could work well there."

"Inspiration," Cassandra confided. "It's most important for an artist to have the proper surroundings. I rather hate to leave Amy and Carl to the mercy of the Lark but perhaps they'll spend more time at the London house and maybe sack her and that revolting brother of hers." The girl's eyes widened. "Oh, I nearly forgot. Gramps was tossing rocks at my window last night at some ungodly hour. He wants me to issue an invitation to you and your secretary, if she's able, to come to the little do for mother on Saturday night."

"I hardly think Miss Sanderson and I should attend. After all, it's a family affair."

"The more the merrier. According to Gramps it's a joyful affair. Probably with mother sitting on a pink cloud and strumming a harp."

"Cass!" Proctor jerked his arm away from her grasp. "That's hardly in good taste."

The straw-colored head drooped and Forsythe asked, "I wonder whether I could see Sir Amyas?"

"He's not here," Proctor told him. "Where did he go, Cass?"

"Amy hustled in to Doctor Beam's to have his burn looked after. I urged him to put a hat and shirt on when he was repairing the dock but he wouldn't listen. He's covered with blisters." She looked up at Forsythe. "I don't know when he'll be back. Amy was muttering something about the amphitheater in Chester so he may have gone over there too."

Forsythe opened his mouth but the front door swung open and Carleton Dancer loped in. He was still wearing cutoffs and desert boots but had yanked his mane of hair back and secured it with what looked like a shoelace. His tanned torso was dripping moisture. "Hi, Carl," his sister said and tugged Proctor toward the door. "I'll drive you into Harper, darling; it's too hot to walk. Tata, Mr. Forsythe."

Carleton fingered his sparse beard. "Can't for the life of me see what Cassie sees in that chap. Wishy-washy. Thought when mother died we'd seen the last of him."

"How do you like the idea of their marriage?"

"Hadn't heard of it. Are they really going to be married?"

"That's what your sister told me."

He shrugged a bony tanned shoulder. "It's Cassie's funeral. Anything I can do for you?"

"I was wondering whether the seal had been taken off the temple's door?"

"Uncle Roland was as good as his word. Inspector Fitzgerald came out yesterday and took it off. Brought back the key too. Like to have a look?"

"If it's not too much trouble."

"No trouble at all." Carleton fished in the drawer of the long table and pulled out a huge ornate iron key. He also extracted a crumpled envelope. "This is for you. When father told the inspector you and Miss Sanderson were down here looking into the murder Fitzgerald scribbled a note and asked us to give it to you. Going to be a hot walk down to the lake. Better wear this." He swept up a straw hat from the litter on top of the table and plunked it on the barrister's head. "Wouldn't want to get sunstroke. Let's go."

They waded through tall grass where George was still waving the scythe around in lazy arcs and apparently not hitting anything. The sun glared down and Carleton slowed his rapid pace to accommodate his companion. "Father was pretty sick last night. Too much sun."

"It doesn't seem to bother you."

"I work outside a lot. All year round."

"Are you still working on the dock?"

"Finished that this morning. Went a great deal faster without father getting in the way. Now I'm working on some lighting for Grandfather Gillimede's ceremony. Hooked up a generator and put up a string of light bulbs the length of the dock. Going to take time to get it working right but it'll keep the old gentleman happy."

The sun glared down and there was not a hint of breeze.

Forsythe's shirt was sticking clammily to his back. "You like to work with your hands?"

"Always have. From the time I was a kid. If I'd been born into a poor family I would have had a better life. Probably been a carpenter or electrician and lived in a council house with a cute wife and a batch of children." Carleton looked dreamily into the distance. "Plant a garden and go to the pub to have a pint and play darts. Take the kids on walks and picnics. Hell of a thing to be wealthy."

"Money can be a curse," Forsythe said dryly.

"And a bore. Traveled all over the world trying to find my niche. Haven't found it yet. Tried the Peace Corps for a time. Labored to teach the simple savage the miracle of birth control and planting crops. Gave it up when I decided they were happier than I am."

"You could take a job."

"And wrench some poor devil's pay away?" Carleton pointed. "See, that's the lighting I put up for grandfather. Neat, eh?"

The future Sir Carleton Dancer had indeed done a neat job. Two strings of bulbs were stretched from a post at the end of the dock to one in front of the temple. A couple of sawhorses and a pile of lumber were directly in front of the door. Carleton wormed his way around them and patted a plank. "Making up a couple of benches for Aunt Pru and the aunts. Can't expect them to stand. Hope the weather holds."

Looking up at the cloudless brass-colored sky, Forsythe said, "I can't see why Saturday shouldn't be a fine night."

Carleton's fine nose quivered like an animal's scenting the air. "Get muggy weather like this and it's usually followed by a hell of a storm." He bent and stuck the key in the rusted padlock. The door groaned open. "Wait a sec. Need flashlights." He fished around in a canvas sack that was leaning against a sawhorse. "Ah, here we are. Should put some lights in the temple but what's the use? Father's going to tear it down soon."

118

They stepped into darkness and swung their flashlights around the interior of the small building. Forsythe's nostrils quivered much the same as his companion's had. The air was clammy and bore a sickening odor. His light settled on a long cement box and he walked over to it. On the top two red candles had guttered in their own wax. A small brass plaque told him that here rested the remains of Sir Godfrey Franklin Dancer, R.I.P. On the far side another cement box stood with its top turned sideways. He flashed the light into the cavernous hole and took a deep breath. This was the source of the sickish sweet odor.

"She was a mess," Carleton said in his ear. "Over three months in there. Body positively squirming with maggots."

Forsythe withdrew his light and his nose from the tomb. He shone the light toward the rear of the temple. On a dais he could see the remains of an oblong glass case. Within the case were two exquisite figurines. Stepping up on the dais he examined them. The green one was a Buddha, the white a delicate figure of a girl. Both pieces were marvelously detailed and the jade was translucent. "The pink ones were even prettier," Carleton told him casually. "Inspector Fitzgerald says they're being held as evidence. He wasn't too pleased that these pieces are still here."

"I hardly blame him. Surely they should be removed."

"They will be when father tears the place down. Katherine's shoulder bag was against the wall. Right there. Her carryall was sitting here." Carleton pointed his torch at the floor. A mass of rusty marks disfigured the white marble and a trail of spots led down off the dais toward the empty tomb. "The police figure she was battered to death right here and the body dragged down to the tomb."

Forsythe stepped down and put a hand under the tilted top of the empty tomb. "How heavy is this thing?"

"Fairly weighty but with the pry bar not hard to move. Leverage, you know. I'd show you but the police still have the bar. More evidence, I suppose." He snapped his fingers.

"Hey, I've got a heavy screwdriver out with my tools. Want to try that?"

Forsythe shook his head. "I'll take your word for it. Wouldn't take much strength, you say?"

"Be a snap. Anyone could do it."

"Cassandra?"

"She's stronger than I am. All that exercising she does. Aunt Bella's strong as an ox and so is Mrs. Larkin." He swung on Forsythe. "Jesus. I see what you're getting at and I don't like it!"

"I don't expect you to but every possibility must be explored. That's my job."

"Thank God I don't have one. Lousy way to make a living."

"This is *not* the way I make my living," the barrister said sharply.

"Sorry, forgot for a moment father and I practically got down on our knees to beg you to do this. Tell you what, Mr. Forsythe, we'll go back to the house and have a drink. I could use one."

"So could I."

They didn't speak on the return trip to the Priory. Both men were engrossed in their thoughts. Forsythe's weren't pleasant. In that dark oriental crypt Katherine St. Croix had assumed a reality to him. Before she had simply been a name and a description. Now she was flesh and blood. Flesh that had been tossed like a piece of garbage into a tomb to rot, blood that had dripped from her body to mark the path that body had taken. Forsythe wondered whose hands had dragged Katherine's body over the marble floor.

CHAPTER TEN

CARLETON DANCER'S QUARTERS WERE ON THE SECOND floor rear and consisted of a room that had obviously once been a lady's sitting room, a bedroom, and a bath. The former sitting room had an ornate ceiling of tinted cupids and flower garlands and the only furniture were a table and two straight chairs in the center of a rug. Three walls were lined with glass cases displaying a multitude of buttons. The air was stifling and Carleton threw up a window before pouring generous portions of Glenlivet. Forsythe noticed that the place was as clean as Cassandra's garret. Not a grain of dust marred the long sheets of glass. "It looks like Mrs. Larkin does do some work here," the barrister said.

"The only area Mrs. Larkin does any work in is father's room and his study. She takes good care of those. Other than that and opening tins for meals, any cleaning is left to George. Cassie looks after her rooms and I wouldn't have servants mucking around in here even if they did offer." Pouring down half of his Glenlivet, he tapped a glass top. "Have a look. I've divided my collection into categories. This is my royalty case."

Royal purple velvet covered the bottom of the case and

on it were clusters and single buttons all with white cards neatly lettered. While Forsythe looked suitably interested, his host expounded. "These jet buttons came from a dinner gown belonging to Catherine the Great. This doeskin-covered button came from a boot belonging to Queen Victoria." He pointed a tanned finger at a tiny gold button with a diamond center. "Wonderful find, this one—a button from one of Henry the Eighth's jerkins."

"Are these authentic?"

"They wouldn't be here if they weren't. And some of them cost a great deal. I've traveled to Paris and Rome and Vienna for them. This silver button once belonged to Marie Antoinette. A very old lady who was a descendant of one of the queen's ladies-in-waiting discovered it in a jar of buttons she had in her attic. The bidding on it was fierce." He moved to the next case. "This is the military segment. Buttons representing every major war and some minor ones. These are the American Civil War, both North and South. This one was from the tunic of Lord Kitchener; and this is the gem of the collection—a button from the waistcoat of Napoleon Bonaparte."

"Extremely interesting," Forsythe said truthfully. "Where do you keep the bone buttons you bought from Miss St. Croix?"

"Over here. I call this my Crime Collection."

The Crime Collection was displayed quite suitably on a black velvet background. These buttons were more contemporary and contained few valuable metals or stones. Enthusiastically Carleton explained. "That pink button came from the cardigan of the fourteen-year-old raped and killed in Manchester last year. This leather one was on the mackintosh worn by that man who went door to door selling magazines and knifing housewives. This—"

"How did you get these?"

"Simple. I watch the papers and get in touch with the families of either the victim or the killer. You'd be surprised what people will sell for a few pounds. Of course there are setbacks. One father of a murdered girl blackened my eye."

Good for him, Forsythe thought. Aloud he said, "And this lot came from Katherine St. Croix. Could you take them out?"

Digging out a ring of keys from the pocket of his cutoffs, Carleton unlocked the case, lifted the top, and picked up the buttons. He poured them into the palm of the barrister's hand. Forsythe prodded at the tiny objects, turning them this way and that. All of the buttons still had pink thread attached and one of them still retained a scrap of a pink cotton material. "Looks like she ripped these off in a hurry."

"Must have cut them right off the blouse without caring whether she ruined it."

Selecting the button with the dangling scrap of material Forsythe held it up for closer inspection. The tiny skull leered with empty eye sockets. "Good detail and carving."

"The best." Carleton's face glowed with fervor. "If she had lived they wouldn't have had much value except as a curiosity but with her death . . . Well, I've already received an offer of five hundred pounds for them. Of course, I wouldn't part with them." He held out a possessive hand and the barrister dropped the buttons into it.

While the younger man carefully arranged the buttons Forsythe read the card below them. In tiny printing it announced that these buttons once belonged to Katherine St. Croix and were cut off her blouse a few hours before she was murdered. Despite the heat he felt suddenly chilled. He said slowly, "Do you realize you are attracted toward death?"

"I beg your pardon?"

"Death and possessions of the dead. Particularly the violently dead. Skulls and those replicas of parts of dead bodies you used with your rock group."

"It never occurred to me before." Carleton locked the case and returned the keys to his pocket. "You could be right." He raised candid eyes to Forsythe. "I do find death and the process of becoming dead much more interesting than the living. At least it doesn't bore me."

When Forsythe returned to the Harper Arms he didn't immediately go to his secretary's room. He had a leisurely soak in the enormous claw-footed tub and donned fresh clothes before he sought her out. Miss Sanderson had been made extremely comfortable. She lay against a pile of pillows and was attired rather nattily in blue silk pajamas a shade darker than her eyes. She was working on a crossword puzzle and the table beside her was heaped with books, an open box of chocolates, and a bowl of fruit. Beside the humble jar of daisies a mass of varicolored roses glowed. In one corner a revolving fan sent ripples of rose-scented air through the room.

Sinking into a chair Forsythe crossed his long legs at the ankle. "You look remarkably cool and well looked after. How's the leg?"

She tugged up a pajama leg and displayed an elastic bandage. "The Sunbeam was around this afternoon practicing his bedside manner again. Rude as ever but he did say the swelling was down and it was coming along as well as could be expected."

"Where did all the goodies come from?"

"Prudence Pyne sent the roses; the missus contributed the fruit; Nell brought up the fan; and our host gave me the chocolates. Probably Mr. Bantam will put them on your bill but it was a nice gesture."

"The books?"

"Nell scurried over to the lending library. Mainly sticky romances so I sent her back for this crossword puzzle magazine. Neighborly people in Harper, Robby."

"So it would seem."

"But I've been so bored—"

"Please. Not that word!"

She put down her pencil. "You've had a boring day?"

"Far from it, but that word was used too often by a young man with the most gruesome tastes. Carleton's managed to turn a button collection into something quite grisly."

"It doesn't surprise me. That rock group is a tipoff to the lad's interests. Think he could have bashed Katherine's head in to add more interest to his collection?"

"Stranger things have happened."

"Rather a weak motive but I'll keep it in mind. Tell me about your interviews."

Forsythe reported in detail. When he'd finished she tapped her thumbnail against her front tooth as she always did when she was thinking, an irritating habit but one that appeared to stimulate her thought processes. Finally she lowered the hand and ticked points off on her fingers. "George Clark is courting Nell and was with her the night of the murder. Margaret Larkin is still in pursuit of a title. Carleton is engrossed in a combination of manual labor and death. That's about it."

"Wrong, Sandy, there's something else." His brow furrowed. "Can't for the life of me pin it down. A remark . . . one of those niggling things you don't notice at the time but strike a chord afterward."

She leaned forward and the crossword magazine slid off her lap. "What remark?"

He shook a baffled head. "That's what I can't pin down."

"Don't worry about it. It will come back if you leave it alone. By the way, what's in the envelope peeking out of your pocket?"

Pulling out the wrinkled envelope he tossed it to her. "A note from the inspector in charge of the case. Gives us a pressing invitation to drop into the station at Chester and confer with him."

She ran her eyes over the sprawling writing. "Inspector

Fitzgerald says we received a glowing recommendation from none other than Chief Inspector Kepesake of the Central Bureau. I didn't think Adam Kepesake thought that highly of us."

"When we were working on those moor murders he certainly didn't but he may feel more kindly since we worked together on the Farquson affair. Adam feels we were the ones who solved the case."

Miss Sanderson bit her lip. "Little does he know he still hasn't the correct solution. Are you going to take Fitzgerald up on his offer?"

"I might as well. We don't seem to be getting far here. I'll drive up tomorrow and—Ah, here is our supper."

The door swung open and Nell entered bearing a bed tray for Miss Sanderson. Mr. Bantam, puffing mightily, carried another tray for the barrister. The maid bent over the bed, snapped down the short legs on the tray, and positioned it. As she moved, the bow in her frizzy fair hair, today a bright red, bobbed frantically. The innkeeper deposited the other tray on the table at Forsythe's elbow. "Eat hearty, folks. Cold food tonight. With the heat and all, the missus don't feel up to cooking a hot supper." He tapped a frosty pitcher. "Iced tea. May hit the spot."

"It will. What's this envelope?"

Picking up the envelope from the tray Mr. Bantam scrutinized it as though he'd never seen it before. "Found it this morning. Meant to catch you 'fore you went out but it clean slipped my mind."

Forsythe looked at the envelope. All it bore was his name in block printing. "Found it where?"

"Slipped under the door. Must have been put there late. Wasn't on the floor when I locked up." He watched Forsythe as he sliced open the envelope and pulled out a single sheet of writing paper. "Something important?"

Refolding the sheet the barrister slipped it back into the

envelope. He glanced up. "You haven't any idea who could have left it?"

"None." Mr. Bantam scratched at the shining dome of his head and muttered, "Queer way to deliver mail."

Forsythe's gaze fastened on his secretary. She was examining a plate of cold chicken and salad with approval. "Mr. Bantam, I'll be driving to Chester in the morning. I don't like leaving Miss Sanderson by herself so much. Could you have a maid stay with her until I return?"

"No problem, Nell's been looking after her. Care to stay with the lady tomorrow, lass?"

The red bow bobbed as Nell nodded. "I'll stay right with her."

Forsythe knew Miss Sanderson was staring at him and avoided her eyes. "If she has any visitors, Nell, don't leave the room. Understand?"

The maid told him she understood and Mr. Bantam caught Forsythe's eyes. He nodded as though something had passed between them and said jovially, "Keep an eye on her myself, Mr. Forsythe. She won't get lonesome, I promise. Now, Nell, come along. Let these folks have their meal."

After the door closed Miss Sanderson said sharply, "Give me that letter."

"I don't—"

"Now!"

He nudged the envelope onto her tray and watched as she opened it. It contained five words in block printing. *Get out or get dead.*

CHAPTER ELEVEN

D<small>ETECTIVE</small> I<small>NSPECTOR</small> F<small>ITZGERALD</small> <small>OF THE</small> C<small>HESTER</small>
police wore half-moon reading glasses that rode precari-
ously on his fleshy nose. The half-moons and the eyes
behind them examined the sheet of paper on the blotter.
"I'll have this checked for fingerprints but I doubt we'll get
any but yours, your secretary's, and Matt Bantam's. Anyone
smart enough to use stationery that can be picked up
anywhere and writes in block printing isn't going to give
himself away by putting his prints all over the note."
Snapping the glasses off, he tapped his chin with their
frames. "Looks like you stirred something up in Harper,
Mr. Forsythe."

"I've been wondering whether this could be a local's idea
of a joke."

"Could be but I'm inclined to doubt it. I think our
murderer just stuck his head up a bit. Going to take his
advice?"

"No."

"Might be a good idea to send Miss Sanderson back to
London."

"Sandy can't be *sent* anywhere. And I doubt she'll go.
She doesn't like being threatened anymore than I do."

Fitzgerald scrutinized his visitor. Robert Randolph Forsythe, Q.C. A much younger man than he'd expected. Looked hardly into his thirties. Soft-spoken and mild-mannered. Tall and slender and dressed with subdued elegance. The inspector mentally draped that slim form in a black silk robe, surmounted the long face with a high gray wig. Forsythe's brilliant reputation as a barrister had preceded him. No, Fitzgerald decided, I really wouldn't want to face this man from the witness box. I also wouldn't be foolish enough to threaten him.

Forsythe was as busy assessing the inspector. Much brighter than Chief Inspector Kepesake, he thought. Carrying too much weight on his big-boned frame. Ginger-colored hair, darker mustache, placid face, sleepy eyes. Good at his job and he knew it.

Fitzgerald tapped the note with the frame of his glasses. "What do you know that warrants this?"

"Quite frankly I'm baffled. As I explained I didn't get any more information than you already have."

"With the exception of George Clark and that business about him taking his girl joyriding that night."

The barrister shifted on the hard wooden seat. "Have you come up with any prior association of the St. Croix woman with any of the suspects?"

"Looked into all their backgrounds and can't find a trace. The only connection Katherine St. Croix or Katerina Padrinski had with anyone in Harper was the few weeks she spent in Miss Pyne's house. Those people and Katerina moved in different circles."

"The Dancers have done a fair amount of traveling. Could they have met the woman in another country?"

"Katerina never made application for a passport. As far as we can find she never left the British Isles. I'm inclined to think the first time she saw any of them was from Miss Pyne's kitchen door and her windows."

"Does that include David Proctor?"

"Proctor was born, raised, and lived his life in London. Katerina was in the city, of course, mainly to have stolen objects fenced. But she seemed to prefer smaller places, towns and villages."

"What about Proctor's background?"

"He was raised by a widowed mother and she doted on him. Only child and his mother used most of her income to give him a musical education. Must have figured her boy was a genius. Appears he was barely adequate. When his mother died he was forced to go to work. Had a number of jobs. Played piano in the lounges of a couple of hotels, sold furniture in an uncle's store, modeled men's clothes for a time, and ended up selling insurance. Not a flaming success at any of them."

"Any romantic interests?"

The inspector fingered his mustache and smiled. "Odd word to use for young people today. Proctor had a number of casual affairs but only one serious one. He and a female model lived together for over a year. Her name was Vanessa Linquist and she was fairly successful. Appeared in television commercials for cosmetics and perfumes and so on. According to their friends Vanessa was the one who broke off the affair. Left Proctor without warning and married a wealthy man who'd been one of her sponsors. It would seem Proctor was crushed."

"Or had a badly battered ego."

"Quite. If he did know Katerina they must have kept it quiet. Neither her associates nor Proctor's knew anything about it."

Fishing in his pocket Forsythe extracted his pipe and a leather tobacco pouch. "What about Katherine or Katerina's background?"

"Makes grim reading." The inspector touched a file folder with a blunt forefinger. "If you like I can give you the gist of it."

"Please."

"One thing the woman always told the truth about was the fact she was an orphan. Her parents were killed in a car crash when she was a little girl and she was put in the custody of an aunt, her mother's sister. The aunt had been a prostitute but as she got older she must have decided there was more money in handling a string of girls than doing the work herself."

"She must have made a wonderful guardian," Forsythe said dryly.

"The aunt put Katerina to work immediately. Quite profitably. An amazing number of men have a taste for very young girls and —"

"How old was the girl?"

"Eight."

"Good Lord!"

"It must have been hell on wheels for the child. Anyway, when Katerina was twelve she ran away from the aunt and ended up in a series of institutions and turned quite naturally to crime. Petty theft, at first. She had a list of juvenile offenses as long as your arm. By the time she reached twenty-one Katerina branched out into extortion. She served two short prison terms and then apparently smartened up. From then on she was up to everything you can think of but she was never again charged. It seemed she had a way of stealing from people and finding some way to keep their mouths shut. Similar to what she tried to use on Cassandra Dancer—threatening to smear them or a relative all over the yellow sheets."

"Yes." Forsythe continued tamping tobacco down in the pipe bowl. He thought of Prudence Pyne and the tactics Katherine St. Croix had used on her. "It certainly didn't work with Miss Dancer."

"She's one in a million. A spunky young woman." The inspector's sleepy eyes glinted with admiration. "We called in our consulting psychologist for a profile on Katerina Padrinski and he tells us it's conceivable, because of the horrendous childhood she had, that Katerina was a woman who hated society and was out to get her revenge. She not only stole for gain but to strike back at people. He says she probably had no sexual drive but achieved satisfaction from tormenting and degrading decent people."

Again Forsythe thought of Prudence Pyne. "What happened to that monster of an aunt?"

"Poetic justice. The aunt was dragged into an alley and several thugs, never identified, beat her to death—slowly. By the time the woman was killed Katerina had a good many connections in the underworld. Doesn't take much to put two and two together."

"For that I can't find fault with Katherine. Seems a fitting end for a woman who'd corrupted her own niece. Any theories about Katherine's death?"

"Ten, Mr. Forsythe. Eight people at the Priory and two people in Harper had the opportunity and sufficient reason to bash her head in. Only problem is to cut the guilty one out of the herd." He laced his hands over his swelling waistcoat. "The way I reason it is this. Katerina, calling herself Katie Parr, weaseled her way into Miss Pyne's house in Harper. She looked over the area and settled on the Dancer family for a future target. She knew they were wealthy and probably thought there would be jewelry and money lying around their house. When she got there she found nothing of value to steal. So she changed tactics and fastened onto Sir Amyas. I should imagine she was going to let him rush her into marriage and then confess her past to him. Sir Amyas would have to pay heavily to get rid of his crooked wife. Cassandra put a stop to that and frightened Katerina into leaving. She left but she stopped off at the temple to pick up some jade for her troubles and one of my ten suspects caught her in the act and bashed her head in."

After two tries, Forsythe got his pipe drawing nicely. He puffed out a tiny cloud of fragrant smoke. "Her body wasn't discovered for over three months. Are you positive she *did* die that Sunday night?"

"You mean could she have sneaked onto the estate at a later date and tried to rob the temple? Everything points against that. In the first place the pathologist managed to locate the remains of broccoli spears in her stomach. Broccoli was served for dinner that Sunday night and—"

"Hardly conclusive. Katherine might have had broccoli at any number of dinners later on."

"True. But—" Breaking off, Fitzgerald consulted his pocket watch, a turnip-shaped affair on a heavy chain. "Thought I was getting a mite peckish. Care to continue this over lunch?"

They lunched at a restaurant near the station house. Inspector Fitzgerald was greeted as a valued patron and they were escorted to a table in a quiet corner. They ordered pints of beer and the inspector finished half of his off at one gulp. "I'm going for something hearty. My wife has me on a diet and all I'll get for supper is cottage cheese and grated carrots. They do a lovely borscht and cabbage rolls here."

Forsythe settled for salad and a Scotch egg. His companion dug into his food and seemed able to eat and talk with no problem. "Where was I, Mr. Forsythe?"

"About to explain the other evidence that points to the date of the murder."

"Right." Breaking off a chunk of bread, Fitzgerald dipped it into the borscht. "The candles sitting on Sir Godfrey's tomb—not ordinary candles and you couldn't pick them up at a store. Lady Dancer had them made up specially for her. Wine red with a gold thread woven into a pattern on them. Those two candles were on the dining room table that Sunday night when the family dined. The next morning Katerina was gone and so were the candles. Mrs. Larkin is positive about that." He waved a hand at a waiter. "Eric, more beer over here."

Forsythe pushed the Scotch egg around. "It does strain

133

the imagination to picture Katherine carrying those candles around and bringing them back at a later date to burgle the temple."

"There's more." Inspector Fitzgerald spread hot mustard liberally on a cabbage roll and cut into it. "After that night Katerina dropped out of sight. Her confederates in London, who disposed of her loot, never saw her again. The daily she had in her flat and the janitor of the building—ditto."

Losing any interest he'd had in lunch, the barrister put down his fork. "London?"

"Chester." Fitzgerald dabbed mustard off his chin. "She kept a flat here for the last couple of years under the name of Kay Parnell. Posed as a well-to-do lady who traveled a lot. The lads went over it with a fine-tooth comb but didn't turn up much except that crime seems to pay. Talk about luxury! Rugs you can sink up to your ankles in and expensive furniture. Two wardrobes in the bedroom. One with cheap clothes, skirts and blouses and anoraks—probably the ones she used when she acted the role of a girl down on her luck. The other one chock-full of clothes that cost a mint. Among other things a fine mink coat and a sable jacket. Some of the gowns had the black and gold label of Madame Helena's."

"Didn't we pass a shop with that name on it in discreet gold letters? The window display featuring only a handbag, gloves, and a scarf?"

"Don't miss much, do you?" Fitzgerald waved for more beer. He sat back and rubbed his bulging waistcoat. "Ah, that hit the spot! Now let the wife bring on her rabbit food. Yes, Mr. Forsythe, that is Madame Helena's. She caters only to the carriage trade and I've heard it costs a pound just to step in and breathe the air. Calls herself—some French word."

"*Couturiere?*"

"That's it. Rather a nice woman."

"You have asked her about Katherine?"

Fitzgerald chuckled. "Operating on the same idea you're

134

mulling over. Women tend to talk to their hairdressers and dressmakers. But Kay Parnell, as Madame Helena calls her, didn't do any talking. If you'd like to have a go at the dressmaker I'll give you my card."

"I think I will." Forsythe waited until the inspector dug out a card and scribbled a few words on it. "There was nothing else of interest in the woman's flat?"

"All there was in the desk was stationery and stamps, receipts for her rent and a few things she'd bought. No letters or checkbooks or even a postcard. She paid cash for everything she bought and for her rent. Suppose she had money squirreled away somewhere, but not there. Besides the clothes and cosmetics there was a jewelry case in her dressing table. Quite expensive stuff in it. Gold chains and a diamond pendant and a couple of dinner rings."

"And that was all?"

"All except what we found in a hidey-hole behind the bed."

"You do enjoy cliff-hangers, don't you?"

The wide mouth below the heavy mustache curved up. "That I do, Mr. Forsythe. But don't get your hopes up. All that was in it was a bundle of clippings from the papers and magazines and a little box containing two pieces of jewelry—antique jewelry."

"By any chance was one of them a garnet ring and the other a cameo brooch circled with pearls?"

"Seed pearls to be exact. No real value there. How did you know?"

It was the barrister's turn to smile. "I should leave *you* hanging but I won't. Those pieces are the property of Prudence Pyne. There were her mother's and Katherine stole them from her."

Rubbing a hand over his thick hair, the inspector frowned. "Miss Pyne didn't mention that to me. Had a feeling she was holding something back. She tell you any other tidbits she withheld from me?"

Forsythe debated and then said slowly, "If Miss Pyne told me anything in confidence that proves to have a bearing on the case, I will put it at your disposal."

"At the proper time, of course," the other man mocked. "I'll hold you to that. Miss Pyne happens to be way up on my list of suspects. Didn't like the way she tried to keep me from questioning that maid of hers. Hung right over the woman while I was talking to her. And Miss Pyne does have a good motive for wanting Katie Parr, as she knew her, dead. That was a pretty filthy trick that was played on her."

"Susan seems to be a highly strung person and she feels guilty about introducing Katie Parr into her mistress's house. As for Miss Pyne being our murderer, quite frankly I can't see it. I'll concede that she could very well have killed the woman with that pry bar but I doubt she could have dragged a body across the floor and hoisted it into the tomb. Miss Pyne is far from young and she has a slight build."

"She also has a hefty maid who could have helped. I could tell Susan was devoted to her mistress."

"Prudence Pyne is not the type of woman who would involve her maid in murder."

"My, you are defensive of this lady, Mr. Forsythe." Fitzgerald's large head bobbed. "First rule in this business is not to get emotionally involved with suspects. Clouds your judgment."

"Tell me more, Inspector," Forsythe said a bit coldly.

"Teach my grandmother to suck eggs, eh? You'll be happy to hear I also have my eyes on the Dancer sisters. Any objections?"

"None. But I can hardly see Miss Sybil being able to do the manual work any more than Miss Pyne could. I suppose you think Miss Bella was her accomplice?"

"She could easily have been. Clear enough Miss Bella is right under her sister's thumb."

"Cats eat birds," Forsythe muttered.

"I beg your pardon?"

"A passing thought. Now, what about the clippings in the murdered woman's flat?"

"All of them concern the Dancer family, dating back to the accounts of Lady Dancer's drowning and her funeral. Katerina had a full collection of data on them, clipped from gossip columns and the society pages. The last one was dated the day before Carleton Dancer picked her up and took her home."

"I'd like to see them."

"Thought you might. I've had copies made and you can pick them up before you leave Chester. Now, Mr. Forsythe, you've drained me dry. Anything you'd like to contribute?"

"I've covered everything I know."

Sighing, the other man wiped a napkin over his mustache and pulled himself to his feet. "When Chief Inspector Kepesake rang me up I had high hopes. He tells me you have an uncanny habit of picking up on tiny things, items no one seems to notice, and building a case out of them. Can't think of some tiny thing, can you?"

"The larder's bare but if anything comes up I'll be in touch."

"Is that a promise?"

Forsythe hesitated. "If you're willing to take my advice on the use of the information, it is."

"Strings attached, but I'll accept them. I'm at a dead end with this case. You off to see Madame Helena now?"

"Yes. Then I'll pick up the clippings and get back to Harper."

"You're worried about your secretary?"

"I made arrangements for her to be looked after but, yes, I'm a bit concerned."

"Matt Bantam seeing to her?"

"And one of the maids who seems a reliable girl."

"Matt's reliable too. Overcharges scandalously but he's a good sort. Brighter than he looks."

In front of the restaurant they parted. The inspector headed back toward the station house and Forsythe walked to the building that housed the shop of Madame Helena, Couturiere.

The reception area was white and gold and chill. On white shag carpeting tiny white and gilt tables and spindly chairs perched. The cool air was faintly perfumed and behind a Louis XIV desk a receptionist, an attractive blonde, raised glacial, appraising eyes. Those eyes took a thorough inventory of the barrister, from his collar to his highly polished shoes, before traveling back up to his face. They noted the cut of the clothes, possibly came to a quick estimate of the cost, and thawed a fraction. "May I assist you, sir?"

He placed his own card and Inspector Fitzgerald's on the desk top. "I'd like to speak with Madame Helena."

She read the cards, picked them delicately up between her thumb and forefinger, gestured at one of the spindly chairs, and disappeared behind white and gold hangings. Forsythe looked the area over. The hangings swayed, and the blonde beckoned him into another room, this one larger but as cool and white and gold although empty of merchandise. Here Louis XIV gave way to deeply cushioned sofas and chairs unholstered in white leather. He followed his comely guide, watching the tantalizing sway of her neat behind, the flash of long silken legs. If this was the receptionist, Madame Helena would probably be intimidating. Behind more white hangings was a stout door and this led to an area that appeared to be the nerve center of the establishment. White shag gave way to worn plank flooring, white paneling to rather grubby green paint. From an open doorway came the whir of machines and behind ranks of sewing machines a number of women wearing blue smocks labored. At the end of the hall the blonde swung open a door and announced him.

The room was small and cluttered. A rolltop desk loomed against one wall; in front of the window a drawing board stood and a long deal table was piled with swaths of cloth and measuring tapes. Madame Helena matched the room. She was short and plump with untidy hair and laughter wrinkles deeply graven around her eyes and mouth. A cigarette was clenched between her teeth and one eye was closed against its smoke. She wore jeans and a plaid shirt and held a scrap of claret-colored velvet.

"A barrister, Mr. Forsythe," she said. "And Inspector Fitzgerald asking me to give you all possible assistance?"

"Retained by Sir Amyas Dancer. To look into the death of Katherine St. Croix, Madame Helena."

"Helena. The madame is strictly for clientele. Any assistance I can give is yours. Not only was Lady Dancer a valued client but she brought me many prestigious ladies including Lady Wabbersley. Do sit down. Take that arm-chair. You'll find it more comfortable than that horrible furniture in the salons. Perhaps a drink?"

Forsythe glanced apprehensively at the array of cut glass decanters filled with a rainbow of colors and she laughed, bringing the wrinkles into play. "I wasn't thinking of a liqueur. The ladies love or pretend to love sticky chocolate and cherry and mint but I happen to prefer double malt."

The double malt was produced from a desk drawer, poured, and Forsythe took a reverent sip. "Where on earth did you come up with this?"

"An aged uncle brews it quite illegally in the Scottish Highlands. Inspector Fitzgerald rather fancied it too." Helena perched on a stool and butted her cigarette in an overflowing ashtray. "You'll want to hear about Katherine St. Croix, or Kay Parnell, as I knew her."

"Please."

"Generally I require references to take on a new client but in her case I made an exception. She spoke and acted like a lady and the fact that she didn't wince at prices helped. In all I made four ensembles for her. Two afternoon dresses, an evening gown, and a heavenly heather tweed suit. It was a pleasure to work on her. For once I could display curves rather than try to conceal bulges. Kay was a fine-looking woman, a brown-eyed blonde, and she had a fabulous figure." Helena spread a hand with short blunt fingers. "And that is all I can tell you."

The double malt sliding silkily down Forsythe's throat was sending pleasant warmth through his body. He leaned back and crossed his long legs. "Surely you must have had some conversation."

"Of course. Mainly about styles and materials." Spreading the scrap of velvet on a knee, Helena stroked the soft nap. "She had excellent taste. I rather wish I had something to confide, some important fact she let slip. But all she said about herself was that she had a flat in Chester and was away a great deal traveling. I gathered she had inherited money and had always had a good life. Education and ease and that sort of thing." Helena raised shrewd eyes from the material. "To fool me she had to be good. I've dealt with women for years and usually I can spot a phoney immediately. Katherine's death was a loss to the theater. She'd have made a wonderful actress."

"She paid in cash?"

"Every time and she also picked up the garments rather than having them delivered. When I found my Miss Parnell was actually the Dancers' Miss St. Croix I was amazed. Also dismayed. If my ladies find I made clothes for a con woman who had the bad taste to have her head bashed in, it may hurt business."

"I see no reason to bring your name into it, Helena. I'm certain Inspector Fitzgerald feels the same way."

Her eyes crinkled with laughter. "And I hope you're right. As I said, Lady Dancer was a valued client and I'm hoping to capture her daughter. Do her wedding gown and trousseau, you know."

Forsythe put his empty glass down and the squat bottle immediately tilted over it. "You've heard about Miss Dancer's engagement so soon?"

"Ah, it is official then. This is a small place, Mr. Forsythe, and I've heard rumors about the impending nuptials for months. Then there have been tidbits about Cassandra Dancer and David Proctor in the gossip columns."

"You've met Mr. Proctor?"

"David escorted Lady Dancer when she came for fittings a couple of times. Handsome young devil. Not my type—I prefer rugged men—but Lady Dancer certainly seemed to dote on him." Helena refreshed her own glass and turned the velvet one way and then the other. "I'd met him before."

"In Chester?"

"London. I did alterations on one of his girlfriend's dresses. For a perfume commercial. Lovely gown, silk and chiffon. She was a model. Can't recall her name."

"Vanessa Linquist?"

"That's it. You're well informed, Mr. Forsythe. Yes, David came and hovered over his Vanessa. He was mad for the girl. I think that's why he was attracted to Lady Dancer. Same basic type. Their features were quite different but both were tall and willowy and graceful, with marvelous dark hair. Vanessa was much the younger, of course." Helena sighed. "Lady Dancer was such a loss. Lovely looking woman and she knew exactly how to dress to display her looks. We used chiffon and velvet and silk for her gowns and kept them simple and flowing. Elegant!"

Forsythe set his glass down again and this time shook his head when the bottle was extended. Uncle's Highland brew was not only delicious but potent. He could feel it down to his toes. "Did you by any chance make the sailor suit for Lady Dancer?"

Her eyes widened. "That was a deep dark secret! But

yes, Mr. Forsythe, to my undying shame I was the one who created that monstrosity. I had no desire to do it but Lady Dancer was too good a customer to refuse. Not only did she swear me to secrecy but she insisted I do all the work on it myself." The laughter wrinkles appeared again. "It's been a number of years since I have done any sewing. All I do now is designing and fittings. Would you like to see the sketch for the infamous suit?"

"I think I would."

She slid open a file drawer and burrowed in it. "Here we are. As you see it was a modified suit of an actual sailor. I nipped in the blouse a bit and used blue velvet for the collar and silk for the red bow. The rest of it was fine white cotton. I used heavier cotton for the cap and put a little blue and red anchor on it. Ghastly thing!"

Forsythe examined the tinted sketch. "Did Lady Dancer tell you why she wanted it?"

"No, she was most secretive about the whole affair. I'll admit I was curious. Her taste was excellent and she *never* wore trousers. It would have been a pity to cover those marvelous long legs. All she said was that it was a surprise and all I asked was whether it would be a pleasant one. Lady Dancer merely smiled."

"Have you told anyone about it? One of your other ladies?"

"Heavens no! In the first place you never discuss one lady's clothes with another. In the second place I'm not exactly proud of creating a tawdry item like this."

"No one could have seen this sketch? Say when it was lying around here?"

She shook her head. "Designs don't 'lie around.' They're kept in that file cabinet. When I leave the room it's locked. And except for staff and police and barristers no one enters this room. The ladies are kept strictly in the salons."

Standing up he handed back the sketch. "I was wondering. I'd like a small gift for a lady. Could you make a suggestion?"

"You're under no obligation to buy, Mr. Forsythe. I was only too happy to try and help."

"I appreciate that but this lady happens to be my secretary who's laid up with a twisted ankle. I thought it might cheer her up."

"In that case . . ." A stubby finger touched her chin. "Lingerie is out. Perhaps a handbag or gloves. I have some marvelous scarves that have just arrived from Paris."

"A scarf sounds fine."

"Then on to the accessory salon. I'll show them myself. Colette, that's the iceberg who mans the desk, is wonderful with the carriage trade; she quite overawes them but is an awful snob."

In her working clothes Madame Helena looked out of place in the white and gold salon. She seated Forsythe on a leather sofa, spread a velvet cloth on the table before him, and turned to a paneled wall. "Where on earth do you keep the merchandise?" Forsythe asked.

"Right here." She pressed a gilt button and the panel slid silently back, revealing rows of narrow drawers. "Trick of the trade, Mr. Forsythe. Keep all the goodies concealed and the ladies feel they're worth the obscene price tags. Now, what is your secretary's favorite color?"

Forsythe mulled this over. "Sandy wears a great deal of green."

"Presto!" Helena opened a drawer. "The perfect scarf."

She draped it expertly on the velvet. "Gossamer silk, hand-painted, observe the artist's signature chastely worked in with the pattern."

The barrister fingered the apple-green silk, admired a spray of pink flowers looking somewhat like cherry blossoms, and nodded. "Sandy will love it."

She grinned wickedly down at him. "And you'll pay three times as much as you would in a department store.

Serves you right for coming to a woman who calls herself madame."

Forsythe found he greatly liked this earthy woman. "How did you come to have a place like this in Chester?"

"The hard way. Long years of being a seamstress and then I met a very generous old gentleman who took a fancy to me. We were extremely close. He insisted on backing this store and lo and behold, Helen became Madame Helena. Lady Dancer was the one who got this shop off the ground. She went to Paris a couple of times a year for her clothes but she dropped in here on impulse and found I could design what she wanted without having to make a trip so she brought more carriage trade and Madame Helena became a minor celebrity."

While Helena had been chatting she had whipped out a black and gold box, nestled the scarf in white tissue, tucked in a sachet, and handed the box to Forsythe. "Brace yourself, Mr. Forsythe. I will now tell you the price."

He winced at the figure and she laughed and accepted the wad of five and ten pound notes. Then she escorted him through various hangings back to the lair of the blonde ice-maiden. At the sight of the box in the barrister's hand the woman rose gracefully and opened the door for him. Helena stuck out a hand. "I'm sorry I couldn't have been of help."

"Oddly enough, I think you have been."

She raised her brows. "Give me a hint?"

"Not yet. It's . . . nebulous."

"In that case come back when you crack the case and we'll have more of uncle's double malt. You can tell me all and when you're quite tiddly I'll sell you a gown for your secretary."

He smiled down at her. "Helena, even uncle's brew won't get me *that* tiddly."

CHAPTER TWELVE

T HE PUBLIC SALOON OF THE HARPER ARMS WAS DOING A roaring business. Matthew Bantam was drawing pints at top speed and Annie, the buxom dark barmaid, was whipping around with plates of salad and cold cuts. As Forsythe made his way to the bar he caught snatches of conversation. Close to the door two young men clad in identical violet pants and matching shirts were in intimate but shrill conversation. The blond one was telling his dark companion, "I grant you Evelyn has a wonderful *body* but, my dear, he can be so *madly* beastly. Why just yesterday he said to me . . ."

Passing a table surrounded by husky young women in shorts, hiking boots, and knapsacks Forsythe caught a storm of words. All the women wore skin-tight T-shirts and none of them favored bras. Forsythe squeezed in beside the checker table and nodded at old Bob. Bob didn't nod back. His ancient but lecherous eyes were busily assessing the unfettered breasts of the hikers. Mr. Bantam busily worked the taps and told the barrister, "He's at it again. Always after the lasses! How was Chester, Mr. Forsythe?"

Forsythe told him all seemed to be in order in that city and asked whether there had been any visitors for Miss

Sanderson. Mr. Bantam opened his mouth but Forsythe caught a whiff of exotic perfume as an arm wearing a gold bangle thrust two glasses past him. "Two more gin and tonics, dear. And just slip a couple of cherries in. Toddy and I are *wild* for cherries."

The innkeeper served the gin and tonics with genial tolerance and told the barrister, "Three people, Mr. Forsythe. Miss Bella Dancer and Miss Pyne both wanted to see Miss Sanderson but I told them the lass was resting. Miss Bella left a box of cookies for her and Miss Pyne a jar of plum preserves. Mr. Proctor dropped in to inquire about her health but didn't ask to see her."

The perfume and gold bangle withdrew and a mild odor of perspiration and a plump freckled arm took its place. Forsythe was aware of something warm and soft and pneumatic pressing against his elbow. The girl was nearly as tall as he and much broader. She had red hair cropped short and rather nice eyes. As the innkeeper drew the bitter those eyes examined Forsythe, the breast continued to nudge him, and she gave him a wide smile. The smile was a disappointment. Her teeth were poor. On the barrister's other side Bob was craning his neck to have a closer look. Mr. Bantam gave the girl the pints and old Bob a crack over the bald head. "Down and stay down or out you go!" he roared. He lowered his voice. "Can hardly blame the old devil though. Talk about big bazooms! Now, Mr. Forsythe, I think you'd do better to tell me what was in that letter. Something is worrying you."

Remembering the inspector's words about the innkeeper, Forsythe came to a decision. Keeping his voice low enough so the hum of conversation covered it he told Mr. Bantam what had been in the note. Mr. Bantam shook his large head. "Figured it was something bad. Might be best to get the lass out of here. Hate to lose her but that don't sound good."

"Sandy won't go. Mr. Bantam, could this be a local's idea of a joke?"

"Was going to deny that right off but you never can tell about people. Even people you've known all your life. Remember a butcher we had here at one time. Nice little chap. Came in every night regular for his pint. Quiet and polite. Took his meat cleaver to the boy who done deliveries 'cause he got the idea the boy was making eyes at his missus. Never can tell what goes on in another chap's head." The innkeeper mulled over the mysteries of other people's heads while he filled glasses and handed them out. The robust hiker was back, this time on Forsythe's other side. Her tankards dropped on the counter with a clatter and she shrieked. Mr. Bantam left his taps and bent over the counter. "What's up then?"

"He's got his hand on my—" She pointed at the aged hand clutching the bulging rear of her shorts. "The dirty old bastard!"

Bantam drew himself up and his face reddened. Apparently it was all right for him to criticize old Bob but he wasn't taking it from anyone passing through. "No dirty talk, lass, and he don't mean no harm. Can you lend a hand, Mr. Forsythe?"

Forsythe lent a hand. He pried the aged fingers loose from the girl's fat behind, took the reluctant oldster to a safer seat beside the fireplace, and returned to buy him a pint. Mr. Bantam refused the money. "On the house." As Forsythe deposited the bitter in the surprisingly strong hand of old Bob, Bantam bellowed, "One more time and out you go, Bob! Sit there and don't touch no one." As Bob ducked his head and sampled his pint, the innkeeper said slowly, "No need to trouble about the lass, Mr. Forsythe, long as she's in the Harper Arms. No harm come to her here. You going up now?"

"Yes. I want to see Sandy before I bathe and change."

147

"Won't find her upstairs. She's down in the snuggery with Nell seeing to—"

"She came *down?*"

" 'Bout an hour ago. Old Bob lent her his spare cane and down she come. Nell and me helped her on the stairs. Tried to tell her—"

Forsythe was away, down the hall, and slamming open the snuggery door. Miss Sanderson, comfortably ensconced on the leather sofa, glanced up from a magazine. "Just what do you think you're doing?" he demanded.

"Calm down, Robby, I—"

"I worry about you all day and here you are walking down the stairs. The doctor told you—"

"She done nothing wrong, sir." Nell leaped to her feet. "Doctor says she can come down if she's careful like. I heard him." The maid giggled. "Miss Sanderson talks to him so funny, sir. Called doctor her little sunbeam and he *smiled.* Then she says he better watch out, he keep doing that and word'll get around he's lost his bedside manner and doctor burst out laughing. Never saw doctor laugh before!"

Forsythe dropped a manila envelope on the table. "All right, ladies, it appears I'm in the wrong. But I've a hunch, Sandy, you wheedled your way down here." He took the deep chair the maid had vacated. "Be a good girl, Nell, and have Mr. Bantam pour a very large neat Scotch for me."

"And an even larger one for me, Nell," Miss Sanderson said. She sniffed. "You smell like a distillery, Robby."

"Courtesy of a Highland uncle." Robby tossed the black and gold box into his secretary's lap. "You don't deserve this."

"Madame Helena! How thoughtful of you." Miss Sanderson ripped the cover off like a child opening a Christmas present. "Simply stunning! A signature scarf." She drapped apple-green silk over the lapels of her dressing gown. "What ever possessed you, Robby?"

"An impulse. I was interviewing Madame Helena and thought of you tucked up in your bed."

"Just what did she have to do with Katherine St. Croix?"

"She designed some clothes for her and—"

Miss Sanderson leaned forward. "As the Red Queen said, begin at the beginning and go on to the end."

"Did the Red Queen actually say that?"

"If she didn't she should have." Miss Sanderson accepted a tall glass from Nell and took a deep swallow.

Nell handed another glass to the barrister. "Would you like a little snack with this, sir?"

Miss Sanderson shook her gray head. "Better not, Robby. I understand the missus is preparing steak and kidney pudding for supper."

"I'll wait for supper, Nell." Forsythe didn't speak until the door closed and then he turned to Miss Sanderson. "I spoke to Inspector Fitzgerald and showed him the note."

"What was his opinion about that?"

"Similar to ours. Someone feels us breathing down his or her neck and would like very much for us to vanish. Now, Sandy, kindly let me tell you this my own way."

Forsythe was still detailing the conversation to his secretary when supper was served. As they ate he finished reporting his interview with the dressmaker. Miss Sanderson shoved away her empty plate and tapped a thumbnail against her front teeth. "You told Madame Helena she had helped and for the life of me I can't see how. She told us nothing we hadn't already heard."

Refilling his coffee cup, Forsythe added sugar and cream. "Bounce some ideas around, Sandy."

"Very well. Fitzgerald is correct. There are ten people who had motives and opportunity. None of the ten can account for their movements the night of the St. Croix woman's death."

"The opportunity we don't have to go into. Tell me the various motives."

"What about physical abilities?"

He rubbed his chin. "We'll take it for granted that the two women who don't have the necessary strength—Prudence Pyne and Sybil Dancer—worked with the maid Susan or Bella Dancer. Start with the suspects with the weaker motives."

"David Proctor. I can't stand the man and I'd love it to be him but I can't see the reason in his case. Maybe he simply was walking, saw Katherine sneaking into the temple, found she was stealing, and bopped her over the head. We know Prudence's motive and I won't go into that. Sybil . . . she may be eccentric but she has a strong sense of family. Sybil could have been outraged to find Katherine desecrating her ancestor's crypt."

"Good reasoning so far, Sandy. Carry on."

"The housekeeper, Mrs. Larkin. She obviously felt Katherine was a threat to her and wouldn't have wanted her to marry Sir Amyas. She could have killed Katherine to get rid of a rival."

"And brother George?"

The clicking sound increased in volume. "Have to be tied up with his sister's welfare, Robby. Plus the fact that Katherine obviously appealed to him." Her thumb dropped away from her mouth. "Maybe George Clark found Katherine in the crypt, made advances, and when she laughed at him picked up the bar and let her have it."

Forsythe chuckled. "Nothing wrong with your imagination. Next suspect—Sir Amyas."

"Well, Katherine did lead him down the garden path. Had the old chap mad for her and when he found her burgling the crypt, reacted violently. Only trouble is *he* was the one who rooted her body out and called us in. His son was right when he said the body wouldn't have turned up for years if his father hadn't gotten that idea about an amphitheater." She made a helpless gesture. "I simply can't work Sir Amyas in."

150

"How about Carleton Dancer?"

"I rather like him as the murderer. The boy may have decided it was time to have a taste of death at first hand. Perhaps it was because Katherine had led him on too. Yes, Carleton is one of my favorite suspects."

"And the other is Cassandra."

"Definitely." Miss Sanderson glowed with enthusiasm. "Strong motive. She'd gotten the goods on Katherine, forced her to leave. Suppose she found the crook lifting the family jade? I can *see* Cassandra bashing Katherine's head in."

"Only one left. Horace Gillimede."

Miss Sanderson slumped back against the pile of pillows. "Damned if I can work him in. Oh, I suppose I could rave on about him struggling with the devil in Katherine's soul and then finding her sinning in the temple but it won't wash. Robby, if Horace didn't lay a finger on either his wife or her lover when he caught them in the act I can't believe he'd hurt Katherine St. Croix. There's no violence in that poor old man."

"You know better than that, Sandy. There's potential violence in all of us."

Miss Sanderson was looking morosely into the cold hearth. "So there is. But we only go round and round. Any of them could be guilty as hell but how to figure which one. We're back where we started, Robby."

"No, we're not, Sandy. Consider this. Is it possible we're working from the wrong end of the whole business?"

"The wrong end?" She ran long fingers through her neat hair. "Do you mean the wrong motive?"

"Exactly."

Miss Sanderson continued to ruffle her hair up until it was no longer neat. "I give up. If you're trying to tie Katherine in with one of these people before she came to Harper I think Inspector Fitzgerald rather cut the ground out from under you."

151

"Katherine came to Harper not once but twice, Sandy."

"So she did. But . . . those clippings! Have you gone through them?"

He picked up the large envelope he'd thrown on the table and opened it. Taking out a sheaf of papers of uneven sizes he divided them into two lots. "I haven't had time. We'd better look them over now. You take the early bunch, I'll take the later ones."

For half an hour all that could be heard in the small room was the ticking of the clock and the rustling of stiff paper. They were interrupted once, by Nell, who gathered up the supper dishes and tiptoed out, closing the door softly behind her. Finally Miss Sanderson tossed the copies of the clippings down. "Waste of time. Bloody hell!"

"Your aura's turning red again." Forsythe grinned, leaned back, and started packing his pipe.

"According to Miss Sybil you were a wise old owl in your last life. Act like one."

"What conclusions have you drawn from Katherine's secret cache?"

"Only that she researched the Dancer family thoroughly before she arranged for Carleton to pick her up and take her to the Priory. Katherine started this collection in August of last year. Every reference to the Dancer family in the Chester and London papers was clipped. She had five accounts of Lady Dancer's death, more of her funeral, scads of junk about the entire family from society pages and gossip columns, any number of newspaper and magazine pictures of them." Miss Sanderson selected a paper and tossed it to Forsythe. "Sir Amyas, his son and daughter, and David Proctor at a bash in London. All I can say is the Dancers look great in evening clothes and Proctor wears his well too. Looks even more handsome in tails. Cassandra is almost pretty with her hair done and swathed in fur and tulle and diamonds. As usual she's holding on to Proctor with both hands."

"Anything else?"

"Oodles. The papers really love the Dancers. Here's Bella becoming president of a meals-on-wheels organization. Seems right in character. Her sister Sybil giving an address to one of those weird societies delving into the supernatural. The address is printed in full and contains a mass of the same terms Sybil used with us. Seeing Souls and auras and whatever. But all that this proves is that Katherine was interested in the Dancers and we already know that."

Reaching for her papers, Forsythe aligned the edges, and started going through them. Miss Sanderson watched him for a few moments and then said impatiently, "I told you everything that's in there."

"Not everything. You omitted one important fact."

"I am *not* playing guessing games," she said wrathfully. "You're on to something."

"Now why would you think that?"

"Because I know you and I know that expression. Your lips crinkled up at the corners like a large cat about to pounce on a mouse."

"Do cats' mouths crinkle at the corners?"

"*Robby.*"

"Calm down. Your aura's verging on bright purple now."

She threw a pillow at him. He caught it, laughed, and tossed it on the floor. "See, even Abigail Sanderson has violent impulses."

"Abigail Sanderson is fast becoming homicidal. You know who murdered Katherine St. Croix, don't you?"

"I believe I do." He sobered. "But there's not a shred of evidence that will stand up in court. Unless we do something extremely sneaky and underhanded this murderer is going to get away clean."

"You're saying we must lay a trap."

"Exactly."

"Give me a hint."

"In a moment I'll tell all. But for now I'll tell you this. Tomorrow is the first day of August. Tomorrow night I'm attending Horace Gillimede's little service—"

"And so am I."

"You can't, Sandy. The memorial service is to be held down at the lake. It's a long rough walk. Your ankle won't—"

"I'll be there if I have to crawl."

He sighed. "No sense in arguing. Knowing you it's useless. Now, you keep off that foot and I'll do the legwork. Tomorrow I'll have to see all of our suspects either in the morning or the afternoon. It won't take much of their time. I'll ask only one question. If the answers bear my theory out I'll have to enlist an ally."

Miss Sanderson's face had brightened. "Now you can tell all."

"I'll begin at the end. Sandy, how mad is mad?"

CHAPTER THIRTEEN

T HE FIRST DAY OF AUGUST DAWNED WITH A BRASSY cloudless sky and heat pressing down like a stifling blanket. Nonetheless the villagers eyed that sky and shook their heads. Old Bob wasn't at his usual place at the checkerboard and when Forsythe questioned the innkeeper he shook his head. "Storm brewing up and old Bob's scairt out of what wits he's got left by a summer storm. Says they're worse than the ones in the winter."

"There's not a cloud in the sky, Mr. Bantam."

"Wait and see. Can smell it in the air. Shame, Mr. Forsythe. Spoil your visit."

Forsythe smiled expansively. "On the contrary, it may make it."

Leaving a puzzled innkeeper he went on his rounds. In Harper he saw Miss Pyne and David Proctor for only moments a visit. His trip out to the Priory took the rest of the afternoon. When he left the last person he saw there, Horace Gillimede, and pointed the hood of the Rover back toward the village, he could discern a haze moving in from the west. By sunset a stiff wind was blowing in from Wales, herding ominous dark clouds before it. Neither the barrister nor Miss Sanderson had much appetite for supper. Leaving the table Miss Sanderson hobbled on Bob's extra cane to a window. "Going to be a dirty night, Robby. Do you think Horace's service will be canceled?"

"Not a chance. But I would urge you to reconsider going out there."

She echoed his words. "Not a chance. What time does the shindig start?"

"On the dot of midnight. We should be out there around eleven. Better wrap up well."

"It's a good thing we stuck our macs in. We're going to need them."

And they did. By the time they stepped out of the car the wind gusted around them, driving their raincoats against their bodies. They were admitted to the house by Cassandra, clad in jeans and a heavy sweater. Closing the door against the blast, she told them, "Awful night. I tried to talk Gramps into postponing this deal but he couldn't be budged. Come hell or high water mother is to be honored. Come into the drawing room."

The drawing room was of magnificent proportions with a high vaulted ceiling, but it was as unkempt as the hall. The baronet was sitting, looking morosely into the dusty fronds of a palm on the hearth. His long lock of hair had been plastered down over his bald spot and he wore a checkered jacket and plaid trousers. The only other person there was David Proctor. He was modishly garbed in a fawn-colored raincoat with large tortoiseshell buttons marching up the front. It looked new and Forsythe decided it must be another item from his trousseau.

Seating Miss Sanderson, Forsythe asked, "Where are the others? Are they going to be here?"

"There'll be a full house," Sir Amyas told him. "Horace is down at the lake and Carl and Mrs. Larkin and George are with him. Prudence is spending the night with my sisters and they'll walk from the Dower House to the lake."

"Shouldn't we start down?"

Cassandra shook her head and the pigtails bobbed. "Carl will let us know when all is ready. I don't want David out in that wind too long." She perched on the arm of her fiancé's chair and captured his hand. "Darling, I do wish you would skip this. You'll catch your death."

"For God's sakes, Cass! Will you stop fussing? I'm not made of glass."

"Your chest. You know—"

He turned away from her and yanked his hand free. "You're worse than the Widow Hawkins."

She draped an arm around his shoulders. "Don't snap so. I only want you in fine fettle for our wedding."

"Wedding?" Sir Amyas jerked his head up. "Oh, that's right. You did tell me. I do hope you're not planning one of those huge affairs with ushers and—"

"Dear Amy." His daughter looked indulgently at him. "You never listen, do you? I told you David and I are going to sneak away and you won't be troubled with having to put on tails and marching me down the aisle."

Proctor managed to look both reproachful and petulant. "You *did* give us your blessings, sir."

"Of course I did, my boy. Glad to see Cassie so happy. As they say, it is better to marry than to burn." He paused and looked at his future son-in-law. "My head's stuffed with sayings like that and I never know where they come from. Who did *say* that?"

Proctor shook a baffled head and Forsythe hazarded, "The Bard?"

"First Corinthians," Miss Sanderson said crisply.

Forsythe laughed. "I'll bet you could give chapter and verse, Sandy."

"Amazing mind," Sir Amyas said heartily. "Tell you what, Miss Sanderson; you ever give up on Mr. Forsythe, you come and work for me. With your memory and my imagination we'd be unbeatable."

157

The door crashed open and Carleton bounded into the room. His hair had been blown into an untidy mass and he brushed a witch's lock out of his eyes. "All ready to go. The aunts and Aunt Pru have arrived. Flashlights on the hall table. Grab one. Black as the ace of spades."

In the hall they milled around, picking up lights, buttoning their coats. Cassandra produced a woolly scarf in a violent pink color and was wrapping it around Proctor's throat. "I am *not* wearing that thing, Cass."

"Don't be silly, darling. Here, I'll tuck it under your coat and no one will know it's there. It will keep you comfy." She told Miss Sanderson, "He has such a delicate chest, you know."

"We've heard about Mr. Proctor's chest," Miss Sanderson said dryly. "You better go on ahead. Robby and I will be slow."

"Watch your step," Carleton warned and loped off after Cassandra and her fiancé.

Sir Amyas walked beside Miss Sanderson, directing his light on the ground. She hobbled along supported by her cane and Forsythe's arm. "Decent of you to come tonight," the baronet said. "Ruddy foolishness, you know, but we're humoring Horace." As he spoke a jagged streak of lightning rent the blackness, making the hillside momentarily as bright as day. Right behind it a boom of thunder sounded like a barrage of artillery. "On top of everything else there's going to be a downpour. So, my little girl is getting married. Hate to lose her. Cassie handles everything. Nice girl. Not like her mother at all, thank God!"

"Horace seems the only one to truly mourn your late wife," Forsythe said.

"I was glad to be rid of her. Awful thing to say and I wish she hadn't died like that but the woman was like an albatross around one's neck. Dreadful person. Viola had a streak of cruelty, you know. Awful hard on those young chaps she

158

took up. Ah, you can see the lights on the dock. Be careful, Miss Sanderson, bit steep from here on."

Panting, Miss Sanderson clutched Forsythe's arm. He pulled her to a stop and they looked down at the lake. Dozens of light bulbs illuminated the dock area and the people on it. Light reflected on the swells moving against the pilings. The white rowboat bobbed beside the dock like a cork.

"Ruddy insane," Sir Amyas muttered and helped Forsythe guide Miss Sanderson down the hillside.

They finally arrived at the dock and Miss Sanderson sank gratefully on one of the rude benches beside Miss Pyne. On the older woman's other side was Sybil Dancer and then her sister. Forsythe took a place beside his secretary and looked around.

Careful preparations had been made. Directly behind his bench was another with Cassandra, David Proctor, and Sir Amyas seated on it. Behind them the temple loomed, its facade looking rather ghastly in the light. At the far end of the dock Horace Gillimede stood behind a wooden structure that looked a little like a lectern. Behind him and to one side were Mrs. Larkin and her brother. George was muffled to the ears in a sheepskin coat and Mrs. Larkin wore a full-length evening cloak that billowed around her like the wings of a gigantic bat. Near them Carleton was setting up an electric guitar. A blaze of color was at his feet—a wicker basket, looking like a laundry hamper, spilled over with flowers. Cassandra Dancer had done her grandfather proud.

"Look at Horace," Miss Sanderson breathed in the barrister's ear. "I can hardly believe it's the same man. He looks so *clean*."

Horace was not only clean but looked as if he'd stepped right out of the Old Testament. He wore an immaculate white toga that swept to his sandals, his hair and beard blew like silver silk, and his face was alive with an expression of exaltation. A circlet of leaves was bound across his high

159

noble brow. The wind was howling but Horace's rich voice soared over it. "Friends, relatives, you know why we stand here tonight in the storm raised by our Lord and Master. We come to honor Viola Gillimede Dancer who now is handmaiden for our God." He raised his face toward the storm-racked sky and right on cue lightning zigzagged and thunder rumbled. "Dear child, I know you hear Daddy's voice. I know you look down and see into our hearts. Look deep, my child, and see our love."

Horace lowered his eyes and swept them across the people seated on the benches. "The ceremony begins; those who are able will embark upon the waves and cast their floral offerings into the waters that took my child's life. Those who aren't may cast their flowers from the dock. While the flowers are being strewn we will offer up a prayer and appropriate music will be provided. Prudence Pyne, will you step forward and choose the flowers you deem suitable for your beloved friend."

Prudence Pyne rose and made her graceful and dignified way to the old man's side. Dancing light turned her hair into a cap as silvery as Horace's. They briefly conferred and as she bent over the basket of blooms Carleton strummed his guitar and Mrs. Larkin and her brother broke into song. They did have good voices—Mrs. Larkin's a soaring soprano, George's a sweet and true tenor. "You'll take the high road and I'll take the low road," they sang.

"Dear Lord," Miss Sanderson whispered. "*Appropriate* music."

"In a way it is," Forsythe whispered back.

Miss Pyne selected a bouquet of sweet peas, stepped to the edge of the dock, and threw them into the waves. She bent her head briefly and then turned and took her place beside Miss Sybil. "Sweet peas are *not* suitable for a peacock," Miss Sybil hissed.

"Hush," Miss Pyne said.

The song ended and Horace beckoned to the singers.

"Margaret Larkin and George Clark, step forward and make your choice." Mrs. Larkin's choice proved to be a spray of green orchids and her brother settled for a handful of daisies. Horace pointed down at the rowboat but both brother and sister shook their heads. They stepped to the edge of the dock while Horace Gillimede, in a magnificent baritone, worked on "Rock of Ages." After they returned to their places, Sybil and Bella were invited to honor the dead. Sybil picked up a bunch of blood-red poppies and her sister mauve gladioli garnished with a gilt bow. Deserting his post Carleton stepped forward to assist his aunts into the boat while Horace extended a hand to help them down the ladder. Neither of the women needed help. They climbed down into the bobbing craft as agilely as primates.

"Ought they to do that?" David Proctor said hoarsely. "It's awfully choppy."

"Dancers are all like seals around water," Sir Amyas assured him. "Strong swimmers and good at handling boats. Besides, Horace has the boat secured to the dock with a stout rope. See?"

"I still don't like it. It makes me queasy even to watch."

While the boat bobbed the younger sister competently rowed it out to the length of the rope and Sybil tossed her poppies and the gladioli into the water. In the meantime George, with Carleton's guitar accompaniment, did a wonderfully moving job on "Danny Boy." "Quite a spectacle," Miss Pyne whispered and both Forsythe and Miss Sanderson agreed.

After the Dancer sisters had safely returned Horace raised his arms and voice. "Cassandra and Carleton, come forward." Carleton and his sister complied, selected flowers, and climbed down into the boat even more agilely than their aunts had. This time Mrs. Larkin undertook a solo of "Greensleeves." Afterward Sir Amyas performed his part in the pitching boat and as he returned to his seat clapped his future son-in-law jovially on the shoulder. "Pitch your flowers in, my boy, and let's get back to the house. It's starting to rain."

After the first tentative drops the heavens opened and the mourners were lashed with gusting wind and rain. Miss Sanderson turned up the collar of her coat and shivered. Forsythe didn't seem to even notice the downpour. He was watching David Proctor's slender back as he strode down the dock. Before he got to Horace's side the old man bent and picked up a tiny nosegay. "For David Proctor who called my child his violet. Violets for my daughter." He appeared to be urging the young man toward the ladder leading to the boat but Proctor was hanging back.

"Amy," Cassandra demanded, "what does Gramps think he's up to? David can't possibly get into that boat!"

"David is young and a man and Horace probably thinks he should. Let them work it out."

"Like hell I will!"

Cassandra started toward her fiancé but before she could reach him her brother and grandfather lifted Proctor bodily and dropped him into the boat. Proctor was shouting and Cassandra screaming and Mrs. Larkin decided to sing a chorus of "Oh, Promise Me." The spectators left their benches and gathered along the edge of the dock. Proctor was hanging to the gunnel with one hand and reaching desperately for the ladder with the other. All he managed to do was push the boat farther away from the dock. Horace lifted a mighty arm and tossed the violets into the bottom of the boat. "Pick them up! Give your violets to my daughter. She's waiting for them."

The young man was frantic with terror. He scrabbled for the flowers and couldn't reach them. He lifted an imploring arm to the people peering down at him. "He's mad!" he shrieked. "He's going to drown me. Help!"

"Yes," Hoarce roared. "I am mad. Mad with grief. You *killed* my daughter!" He brandished his arm again and this time his huge hand clutched a knife. The blade glinted in the swaying lights. "Confess or I will cut the rope and you will perish and vanish beneath the waves!"

Cassandra threw herself upon the old man but her brother hauled her away. "Amy," she screamed. "Help me! Gramps and Carl are crazy. They're going to drown David!"

Her father paid no attention. He bent over the edge of the dock, his eyes intent on David Proctor. Horace lifted the knife over the stanchion where the rope was fastened. "Your last chance, murderer! Confess or die."

Proctor's mouth was moving and his eyes were rolling frantically. They couldn't hear a word he was saying. "Shout!" Horace cried. "Lift your voice so all may hear."

Proctor's mouth writhed and then he threw back his head and bellowed, "I killed Viola! I killed Katherine! For the love of God, save me!"

Horace dropped the knife and turned to Forsythe. "It is over."

"Yes. Get him out of that boat."

In the circle of her brother's arms Cassandra was now standing quietly. Carleton pushed her gently toward their father and Sir Amyas cradled the girl, his cheek pressed against her wet hair. Horace pulled mightily on the rope until the boat nudged the pilings. Carleton swarmed down the ladder, lifted Proctor's limp figure, and started pushing him up the ladder. Bending, his grandfather seized Proctor under the armpits and lifted him as though the other man were a child. He tossed Proctor onto the planking and stood back, his chest heaving.

Everyone but Forsythe was staring down at the wet, bedraggled figure. Forsythe had turned away and was looking up at the shadowed walls of the temple. Three figures were trotting down toward the dock. The one in the lead halted by the barrister's side. "Could you hear?" Forsythe asked.

"Clear as a bell," Inspector Fitzgerald told him. He

163

gestured at his sergeant and constable. "Get him up to the house, lads. The rest of you people get up there too."

Miss Sybil, straightening her turban, raised a haughty chin. "I have sworn never to enter my brother's house again."

"Tonight you will," Fitzgerald told her grimly.

"Well, perhaps I can make an exception in this case. Bella, in Mr. Proctor's next incarnation he will be a weacock."

"What's a weacock, Sis?"

"A cross between a peacock and a weasel. Do you agree, Mr. Forsythe?"

The barrister put a comforting arm around his secretary's shoulders. "I couldn't agree more, Miss Sybil."

They watched while the policemen lifted the weacock and, half carrying him, bore him up the hill in the direction of the Priory.

CHAPTER FOURTEEN

By the time Forsythe and a wet, bedraggled, and thoroughly exhausted Miss Sanderson had climbed back up the hill and entered the drawing room of the Priory, Cassandra had recovered from shock. She was standing, arms akimbo, wrathfully facing Inspector Fitzgerald.

"Was this atrocious charade your doing, Inspector?"

"No, Miss. Mr. Forsythe rang up this morning and told me to be down at the temple tonight before midnight. He said I might hear something of interest in the St. Croix case."

The girl swung on Forsythe. "So it was *you*. And you had Amy and Carl all primed to help Gramps."

Seating his secretary he helped her remove her sodden raincoat. "Not primed. I merely asked them not to interfere."

Carleton gave his sister a satisfied smile. "I enjoyed helping grandfather, Cassie. Never did like Proctor."

Paying no attention to him Cassandra spun around. "And you, Gramps. How could you do this?"

Horace straightened the wilted leaves over his brow. "Robert came to me this afternoon as an emissary of our

Lord and pleaded for my assistance. He told me he *knew* David was a murderer and had killed my child but he couldn't prove it. Robert said the only way justice could be done was to force a confession from the sinner."

"*Force.*" The girl returned to her attack on the policeman. "David would have said *anything* to get out of that boat. This is confession under duress. It will never stand up in court."

Fitzgerald's sleepy eyes looked benignly at her enraged face. "I realize that and so does Mr. Forsythe. But Mr. Proctor does have some explaining to do."

"David will *not* say a word. I'm going to ring up Willis Seton and we'll blow this whole smelly affair to smithereens."

"Sit down and shut up, Cass." Proctor slumped in a chair, moisture beading on his raincoat, his dark hair plastered to his head. "For the past year I've lived in hell. I'm glad it's over. I'm prepared to make a statement. But first I'd like to ask Mr. Forsythe a question."

"Ask away," the inspector told him.

"I thought I'd covered my tracks. How did you get on to me?"

"With difficulty," Forsythe told him. "We had ten suspects and it seemed impossible to single out the guilty one. For a time I struggled with Katherine's murder, trying to find the person with the strongest motive for it. But in each case the motive was too weak. After all, if one of you had discovered Katherine looting. the temple it wasn't necessary to kill her. The natural reaction would have been to call the police and have her charged. Both the inspector and I tried to establish some previous link with the dead woman and one of you but there was no link."

The barrister templed his fingers. "Three rather odd things kept reoccurring. The costume Lady Dancer was wearing the night of her death, a hundred pounds in Katherine's carryall we couldn't account for, and the

166

resemblance between Vanessa Linquist, a model once loved by David Proctor, and Lady Dancer."

Cassandra had sat down but she didn't shut up. "Bunk! Mother's sailor suit was simply a foolish whim. Katherine could very well have brought that money with her. As for the resemblance between this model and my mother . . . men do tend to fall for the same type of woman, you know."

"No, Miss Dancer, Katherine wouldn't have brought a hundred pounds to a house in which she was posing as a penniless orphan. In a way the woman was an artist. She kept a special wardrobe of cheap clothes for her roles and she was too shrewd to bring money into a house when it could have been discovered by a servant. Katherine St. Croix acquired that hundred pounds while she was in this house and the person who gave it to her wasn't about to admit it. Miss St. Croix was an old hand at extortion. Ergo, she was blackmailing one of you."

Forsythe looked at Cassandra and she stared back with hostile eyes. "I asked you a question this afternoon."

"You asked me whether I had ever talked about mother's sailor suit with anyone but a relative or David or Aunt Pru. I said no. Gramps made us swear on the Bible we wouldn't tell about it and the only other people I discussed it with were you and Miss Sanderson. And I did that became Amy asked me to speak freely with you."

"That is exactly what all the rest said too. Yet—" Forsythe turned to his secretary. "Sandy, will you read that excerpt from the interview with Horace Gillimede?"

Twisting sideways Miss Sanderson pulled a notebook from her pocket and leafed through it. " 'I recounted my own sins and she commiserated with me. There were tears in her eyes as we spoke of my poor dead wife and she told me she understood why the shock had been so great when my daughter went to her judgment clad in men's attire.' "

Forsythe nodded. "The 'she' Horace was speaking of

was Miss St. Croix. If none of you talked, how did Katherine know about Lady Dancer's outfit?"

"Simple." Cassandra spat the one word. "Gramps told her all about it when he was raving on about his sins."

Her grandfather's silvery head shook. "No, my child, I didn't mention it to the woman. At the time I was so upset I didn't notice what she said. Katherine didn't learn about it from me."

"That is what Horace told me this afternoon," Forsythe said.

Cassandra was frowning. "There're other ways."

"Name one."

"The dressmaker who made up the suit . . . she might have babbled."

"That occurred to me and when I found the woman had made clothes for Miss St. Croix also, I thought the dressmaker might have told her. Or that Katherine, who was an accomplished criminal, had gone through the records at the establishment. But it was demonstrated to my satisfaction that Katherine hadn't found out there."

Miss Pyne bent forward. "Katie found out while she was at my house. I can see that now."

Forsythe nodded. "When you combine the interest Katherine had in the Dancer family and her nocturnal absences from your house, Miss Pyne, you can understand that she wasn't *told* about the sailor suit, she *saw* it. Last year, at this time, Katherine St. Croix must have been roaming these grounds and she must have seen Lady Dancer die. She also saw who was with Lady Dancer when she died. I came this far in my reasoning and then I hit another snag."

"What was that?" Sir Amyas demanded.

"Katherine waited for eight months to return to Harper and worm her way into your home. Why didn't she start blackmailing immediately? The only answer to that was that the person involved in Viola Dancer's death didn't have

168

enough funds to make it worth Katherine's while. That neatly disposed of half the suspects at one time. Sir Amyas, his son and daughter, his sisters—all are wealthy. I had to look at one of the other five, the ones without funds."

The lump in George Clark's throat jumped convulsively. "Maggie and me."

"That would also include me," Miss Pyne said.

Forsythe nodded. "And Horace Gillimede and David Proctor. While Katherine St. Croix waited she collected every reference she could find to this group of people and made a collection of newspaper clippings." He leaned back and closed his eyes. "You can picture the woman like a pretty blonde spider sitting in a web waiting for her fly to fatten." His eyes snapped open. "The moment I examined those clippings I realized the identity of the murderer. Horace, Miss Pyne, George and Mrs. Larkin, were not mentioned. But David Proctor—he was photographed with the Dancer family, gossip columnists were linking his name with Cassandra, rumors were drifting about their impending marriage. At the time of Lady Dancer's death Mr. Proctor wasn't worth blackmailing. But now he was to marry a girl not only wealthy in her own right but with expectations of an inheritance from her father."

Miss Sybil's turbaned head bobbed. "And the snake Katherine came to the Garden of Eden."

"She came with two ideas. To prepare her blackmail victim to be sucked dry and to pick up any item of value she could find. Katherine discovered there was nothing in the house to loot so she turned her attention to Sir Amyas. She would have been delighted to marry him and milk him dry too. But Cassandra took steps against the woman and forced her to leave. Katherine St. Croix then decided to pick up what money she could from David Proctor and also to steal the jade from Mandalay. What she got, as we know, is death."

Forsythe leaned back wearily and Inspector Fitzgerald

cleared his throat. "Now, Mr. Proctor, are you ready to make a statement?"

"Don't," Cassandra implored. "Please, David, let me call Willis Seton."

"I told you to shut up." Proctor's hair had dried and he shoved it back from his temples. A lock fell forward over his rounded brow. He looked from the inspector to the sergeant who held a pencil poised over a notebook. "I want all of you to hear this confession. I want you to know that I was with Viola when she died."

"David," Sir Amyas said softly. "Viola was going to divorce me and marry you. Why?"

Proctor's mouth snapped open and for a moment it looked as if he was going to order the baronet to shut up. Instead he said, "The morning of Viola's birthday she rang me up. Viola asked me not to come to the dinner but to meet her near the temple at eleven that night. I was delirious with joy. I *loved* her. She'd given me to understand that soon we would be together for the rest of our lives. I was there early, sitting in the moonlight, so happy. She came, dressed in her sailor suit, and pirouetted in front of me. She told me she'd had it made especially for me. I took her in my arms but she broke away and danced down to the dock. Viola said she wanted to talk to me on the water, that we had one last thing to do. We must break through our morbid fear of water."

The young man paused and looked into space. "I didn't want to get into the boat but the water was calm and I couldn't let Viola believe me a coward. So I took the oars and she sat opposite me in the bow of the boat. She took off her little white cap and threw it in the bottom of the boat. Then she ran her fingers through that marvelous silky hair and she smiled at me. She told me she'd come to a decision and she had a sacrifice to make. Viola said her father would be shattered by a divorce and there were Cass and Carl to consider as well as the aunts. She said it was her *duty* to stay with her family." Proctor gave a bitter laugh. "Duty! I

170

knew what she meant. Viola preferred to be Lady Dancer, not Mrs. David Proctor. I saw her as she was—cruel, capricious, shallow. But I loved her and I argued, trying to change her mind. She was adamant."

Proctor looked not at Cassandra or the Inspector but at Forsythe. "You mentioned Viola's resemblance to Vanessa. Yes, they looked alike. Vanessa said she loved me and married a wealthy man. Viola said she loved me and was going to stay with a wealthy man. I couldn't stand it."

"So you chucked the other peacock out of the boat," Miss Sybil said jovially.

"I did *not*. I said I would stay on in Harper and hoped she would change her mind. Viola flew into a fury. She jumped up as though she'd forgotten where she was. She screamed that she wanted me out of her life and out of Harper. She said she would go to the parents of my music pupils and tell them to discharge me. She said she would have Mrs. Hawkins throw me out of her house. She was rocking the boat and I was terrified she might upset it. I stretched out an arm to her and she must have thought I was going to strike her. Viola backed away and her legs caught on something and she fell into the water." He buried his face in his hands. "She went down like a stone."

"And you rowed back to shore and then overturned the boat and set her cap adrift," Inspector Fitzgerald said mildly.

"I was afraid her body wouldn't be found. I left them as . . . as markers."

Cassandra's close-set eyes were distressed. "David, when I rang you up the next morning you pretended to search for mother; you acted so worried. How could you?"

"I couldn't tell the truth. It was too late for that. Cass, I've gone through hell!"

"Then, Mr. Proctor, you were approached by Miss St. Croix," Fitzgerald said.

"Shortly after Viola's death, Cass told me she loved me.

Up to that point I'd been so involved with her mother I hadn't even noticed Cass. I wouldn't marry . . . I couldn't. I was too heartbroken. But time passed and I started to heal. I thought perhaps Cass and I could have a life together." He took a deep breath. "When Katherine arrived at the Priory I hardly even noticed her either. But she came to see me and told me she had been on the grounds that night and she had seen and heard all. Katherine said at that time I wasn't worth bothering with but now I was in a position to pay her large sums. I told her it had been an accident but she laughed and said she'd tell the police and the Dancer family I'd deliberately drowned Viola. Katherine was horrible; she gloated, I told her I didn't have a pound and she said—"

"She said you'd better raise some money on your watch and cigarette case," Forsythe said.

Cassandra snapped forward. "David," she wailed. "Those things weren't stolen."

"They were pawned and the old devil would only give me a hundred pounds for all of them. On Sunday Katherine rang me up and told me—"

"Ah," George Clark said triumphantly, "that's who the bird was phoning from the writing room."

"Katherine told me that Cass had found out about her past and she must leave the Priory. She told me to meet her at Mandalay that night at eleven-thirty. When I got there the candles were burning and she was breaking the glass in the jade case with the bar. I gave her the money and she tossed it on top of her carryall. There was another bundle of notes already in it. Katherine took out the pink jade and wrapped them up in her underwear. She knelt beside the carryall and pushed the jade in under the money. All the time she was talking. She ordered me to marry Cass and to do it fast. She said Cass had lots of money for both of us. She said I would never be free of her. Katherine's head was bent and her hair

172

fell away from the nape of her neck. It looked so . . . fragile."

Proctor rested his head back against brocade. His face was drained and exhausted. "A red haze seemed to come down over me. When it cleared I was standing over her, the bar in my hand, and her head was . . . Oh God! I'd killed her. I'd gone mad and battered her head in!"

"The best way to kill a snake," Miss Sybil said approvingly.

Inspector Fitzgerald shot a bemused look at the elder Dancer sister and then asked Proctor, "Why did you put the body in the tomb and leave the shoulder bag and carryall exposed?"

"I didn't think the temple would ever be entered and I couldn't just leave her there, sprawled on the floor. I was temporarily insane. I think . . . I must have been trying to give her a burial." Proctor put a dramatic hand over his eyes. "That is all."

"Not quite," Forsythe said crisply. "I had just about given up on this case when I got your threatening note. It was foolish of you to do that."

The hand dropped limply. "What note?"

Miss Pyne touched the barrister's sleeve. "Mr. Proctor didn't put that note under the door of the Harper Arms. I did."

"Why?"

"I wanted you and Miss Sanderson to leave. I can see now I did the wrong thing. But Katie Parr was a demon and I didn't want you to find Mr. Proctor had killed her."

David Proctor's fine warm eyes were wide. "You knew it was me?"

"I guessed. The night that Katie Parr disappeared from the Priory I took a walk. I had just turned in at my gate when I saw you walking down the road from the direction of the estate. It was a moonlit night and I saw you clearly. At the time I thought you had been visiting Cassandra. Then when Katie's body was discovered I realized it had to be you who had killed her. You'd sworn you hadn't left your rooms that night. So I tried to frighten Mr. Forsythe and Miss Sanderson away from Harper."

"And that's where you made a mistake," Inspector Fitzgerald told her. He got ponderously to his feet. "Mr. Proctor, you will please come with us."

"Gladly," the young man said and went with the three officers.

Cassandra collapsed on the sofa, weeping. Helplessly her father patted her shoulder. "Better ring up Sarah and Roland," he told his son. "Cassie needs a woman to look after her."

In record time Lord Wabbersley and his stout wife arrived and scooped up their weeping goddaughter. Soon after, Miss Sybil, without glancing in her brother's direction, took a stately departure with her sister and Prudence Pyne. Mrs. Larkin was fussing around Sir Amyas and he curtly ordered her and George to their quarters. Then the baronet said to his father-in-law, "Better spend the rest of the night with us."

"No." The old man was on his feet. He adjusted a fold of his toga. "I will walk this night beside the lake."

"Grandfather," Carleton said. "You can't go out in that storm."

"Your ears are not keen, my boy. The Lord has calmed the wind and stopped the rain. He raised the storm to unmask a sinner and that work is done." Horace bent a stern gaze on the barrister. "I did as you asked. Was this the Lord's will?"

"David Proctor was involved in the deaths of two women."

"He was and I could not allow Cassandra to fall into his bloodstained hands. But I do not like what I have done this night. I go now to pray for the souls of the dead. I will pray

174

for Viola and for the woman known as Katherine. I will also pray for the soul of David Proctor."

Carleton gazed after the old man. "Crazy as a loon!"

"I find him rather magnificent," Forsythe said.

Sir Amyas said heartily, "And I find your work magnificent. You've cleared the Dancer name. We didn't discuss fees but there will be a check in the post. Goodnight, Mr. Forsythe. Miss Sanderson, remember a position will always be waiting for you in my employ. Carleton, would you show our friends out?"

Carleton led the way into the hall. As Forsythe opened the door the young man held out his hand. On the narrow palm rested a large tortoiseshell button. With childlike pride he told them, "I yanked it off Proctor's coat when we were hoisting him up the ladder."

"You're going to add it to your Crime Collection?" Forsythe asked.

"Yes. It will be the star of my collection."

As the Rover turned back toward the village Miss Sanderson said morosely, "That lad's true vocation is as a mortician."

Forsythe shot a look at her tired face. "Going to take Sir Amyas up on his offer?"

"It might be rather interesting to help erect a Roman amphitheater." She squeezed his arm. "But I think I'll stick with you. You may have the makings of a detective."

"I'm a *great* detective."

"Watch it, Robby! In your next life you could be a peacock." She considered for a moment. "Or maybe a weacock."

CHAPTER FIFTEEN

THE SUMMER STORM CLEARED THE AIR AND PUT AN END TO the oppressive weather. The morning that Forsythe was loading up the Rover was sunny but the air was pleasantly fresh. He lifted his pigskin case into the trunk and reached for his secretary's traveling bag. Her typewriter case fitted in between the other pieces of luggage. As he slammed the trunk lid down Miss Sanderson, carrying only her outsized handbag, came out of the Harper Arms. She was wearing her green linen suit and Madame Helena's silk scarf was tucked into the vee of the jacket. Her ankle was still bandaged but she had discarded the cane. Behind her paced their innkeeper, cradling in his arms a large wicker basket. Old Bob, his eyes fastened on Miss Sanderson's long shapely legs, hovered behind Mr. Bantam.

"Fine morning," Bantam told Forsythe. "Be a pleasant trip back to London. Mind how you handle this basket. Bit tetchy."

Carefully Forsythe positioned the basket in the middle of the rear seat. Then he held the door for Miss Sanderson but she was busy with Bob. Putting a hand on the old man's frail shoulder she dropped a kiss on his bald dome. He grinned from ear to ear. "He won't be fit to live with now," Mr. Bantam complained. "You've fair turned his head."

As Forsythe started the car their host stuck his head in the window. "Come back anytime, folks. Always be a warm welcome at the Harper Arms."

The car clattered over the cobblestones and Miss Sanderson twisted around to wave. The innkeeper lifted a majestic hand and old Bob was brandishing his cane. "Nice people," she told her companion.

"Salt of the earth. Sad to leave?"

"In a way, but I find I hunger for double-deckers and swarms of cars and breathing noxious petrol fumes. I'm afraid I'm not quite ready for a bucolic life. But I will miss some of the people here. While you were busy with Inspector Fitzgerald I had swarms of visitors."

"Any interesting tidbits?"

She smiled. "Oodles. Carleton is planning on renting a salon in London and showing his collection. Seems he plans to use Katherine's bone skulls and Proctor's tortoiseshell button as a special exhibit. He gave us pressing invitations and told me he expects crowds of people out to view them."

"No doubt he'll get them. Morbid types scenting blood. What about his father?"

"Going ahead full speed with the Roman amphitheater. Sir Amyas has made arrangements for Sir Godfrey's ancient bones to be interred at St. Jude. The vicar is going to have a small service and appropriate music will be provided."

"I wonder what selections will be played."

"Probably 'John Brown's Body.' By the way, Sir Amyas sacked his housekeeper and her brother. Seems he finally had a look around the Priory and decided to get rid of them."

"Have they any plans?"

"Nell tells me she and George will be hitched and her old dad is setting them up in a pub. I suppose Mrs. Larkin will tag along to give the place some class and probably drive the newlyweds mad."

"Did you see Cassandra?"

"Oh, yes. She's still has it in for you but doesn't hold anything against me. Figures I'm just the hired help. She told me she intends to 'stand by her man.' Cassandra is arranging for the best legal counsel available. She's also encouraging her David to write a documentary about his little problem with Lady Dancer and Katherine St. Croix. Cassandra feels it will be a best-seller."

Forsythe sighed. "That is probably the truth. And if she feels he'll get off with a light sentence she's right. With that profile, those soulful eyes, and his temporary insanity Proctor will have the jury firmly on his side."

"Did you believe his story?"

"Let's put it this way—David Proctor has the makings of a fiction writer."

"He killed both women in cold blood, didn't he?"

Forsythe guided the Rover over the humpbacked bridge and swung the hood into a right turn. "In Lady Dancer's case it was probably hot blood, practically on the boil. Proctor's ego had already taken a pounding from Vanessa Linquist and when Viola Dancer tried to discard him I should imagine he broke. I can picture him throwing or shoving the woman out of the boat."

"She didn't go down like a stone."

"My guess is Viola thrashed around while Proctor enjoyed. I can see him fending her off with an oar. For once Katherine wasn't lying when she threatened Proctor. She *did* see him murder Lady Dancer. When she blackmailed Proctor she was a dead woman. All he did was wait for a chance to finish her off."

"Which she gave him."

"He came prepared, Sandy. Gloves. That night, as we learned from George Clark, was warm and balmy and Proctor was wearing gloves."

Miss Sanderson's brow crinkled in thought. "For the life of me I can't understand why he didn't take those packets of money."

"They were rather a mess—covered with blood and bits of brain and bone. Too messy for our sensitive young poet. Anyway, Proctor, with marriage in sight, had no need for a trifling amount of money. Why are you looking so perturbed, Sandy?"

"As soon as he's free Cassandra plans to marry the man. Robby, he killed *twice*. What if he decides he wants the beautiful money and not a homely wife?"

Forsythe shrugged. "That happens to be Cassandra's funeral."

"You're rather callous."

"Fatalistic. She knows all about him. Anyway, Proctor's bright and may not try anything too drastic. He may feel you and I are lurking around, waiting for a suspicious death."

"And he'll be right," Sandy said grimly. "Odd, I can't understand the girl. Of all the Dancers she seems the most sensible."

"Cassandra is still a *Dancer*." He patted her knee. "Now, forget about the whole business and tell me what's in the 'tetchy' basket."

"Gifts. Fresh-baked bread and Chesire cheese from Mr. Bantam and his missus. A yummy fruit pie and a pot of jellied veal from Miss Bella. A crocheted doily from Prudence Pyne and a heavy tome all about reincarnation from Miss Sybil. Sir Amyas gave me a gift for you but I'm not to say a word about it until we're back in London."

"Say a word about it, Sandy."

She debated and then said, "He insisted you have that jade Buddha. He—"

"Sandy!" Forsythe pulled the car over to the side of the road. "That's ridiculous! The jade is worth a small fortune."

"I know, but there's no way of saying no to Sir Amyas Dancer."

He looked over his shoulder. "And it's rattling around in that basket?"

"Hardly rattling. All swathed in cotton wool and in a metal box. The best course is to accept it gratefully."

"It will look well on my desk. All right, I'll be graceful about it. I also better arrange for insurance. You can come in and admire it occasionally if you share your bread and pie with me."

"Not a chance."

"Don't be greedy. Tell you what, I'll stop and pick up paper plates and cups and we'll picnic on the banks of some meandering stream. I'll even throw in a couple of bottles of wine."

"Make that nut brown ale and you're on," Miss Sanderson said.

"Done," Robert Forsythe told her.

ABOUT THE AUTHOR

E. X. Giroux is also the author of A DEATH FOR ADONIS
and A DEATH FOR A DARLING. She lives in Surrey,
British Columbia.

Attention Mystery and Suspense Fans

Do you want to complete your collection
of mystery and suspense stories
by some of your favorite authors?
John D. MacDonald, Helen MacInnes,
Dick Francis, Amanda Cross, Ruth
Rendell, Alistar MacLean, Erle Stanley
Gardner, Cornell Woolrich, among many
others, are included in Ballantine/
Fawcett's new Mystery Brochure.

For your FREE Mystery Brochure, fill in the
coupon below and mail it to:

DEADLY MYSTERIES

and only Robert Forsythe knows who-dunnit!

Stories by E.X. Giroux